RUBY'S LOVE SPELL SUMMER

RUBY'S LOVE SPELL SUMMER

❀

Maggie Garnet

iUniverse, Inc.
New York   Bloomington

Ruby's Love Spell Summer

iUniverse books may be ordered through booksellers or by contacting:

iUniverse
1663 Liberty Drive
Bloomington, IN 47403
www.iuniverse.com
1-800-Authors (1-800-288-4677)

ISBN: 978-1-4401-9613-3 (sc)
ISBN: 978-1-4401-9612-6 (ekb)

Printed in the United States of America

iUniverse rev. date: 01/28/10

In this work of fiction, any similarity to names or natures of persons living or dead, or names of places, publications or musical groups is purely coincidental and not intended by the author.

*   *   *

Mexicali Rose original lyrics by Helen Stone, music by Jack B. Tenney; M. M. Cole Publishing Company (1923).

To my Great Grandmother Maria, Grandmother Margaret
and Great Aunt Esther

For the June Solstice Eve's special dream of love, hide the largest pinecone to be found within a satin pouch stitched by your own hand. Slip under your pillow and sleep upon it for one night.

I.

❀

The narrow three-flat apartment building where Ruby lived was on Philadelphia's 12th Street just after it crossed Spruce, with pigeons on the fire escape followed by alley cats stalking the pigeons, and a landlady who snooped through everyone's mail. The landlady, once known as Glorious Gladys in her turn of the century chorus girl days, was more whiny than glorious now and in general a big blathering snoop. Gladys's apartment was on the first floor and, like a henna-haired troll under a bridge, very little slipped past her constantly watchful eye—unless she had been boozing and was sleeping one off.

When the letter came from Ruby's Great Aunt May, there was a slight delay in its actually being placed upon the rickety black lacquered table in the apartment foyer, where all the mail was stacked after secret inspection by Gladys. It wasn't that Gladys stole checks or extorted money from her tenants through whatever juicy tidbits she discovered in their letters, it was simply that she was bored, nosy, and overly obsessed with her landlady role. Fortunately, Ruby's Aunt May was so old-fashioned and respectful of postal communications that she still used sealing wax, and Gladys would not have been able to steam open the letter without breaking the seal. Therefore, when Aunt May's letter did finally did hit the black lacquer table, it was just damp with a partially melted wax closure, but the envelope was still intact. Gladys blamed the letter's sticky condition on the June heat, then added her usual lie that the postman was a lazy Mick and had probably left it in his bag for a few days.

Once she had managed to get past Gladys and her hovering and questioning and fluttering around in a beer-stained peignoir, Ruby sat on the sofa of her neat, bright apartment and broke Aunt May's seal herself. She had a feeling that the letter might just be to wish Ruby a happy birthday on June 17th, this date already having passed earlier in the week—but then again there might be more to the contents. And there was indeed more, in the form of two wispy pressed violets and Aunt May's delicate handwriting issuing both a reminder and a challenge:

As we spoke of this last spring after your dear father's funeral, Ruby Jane, you are now twenty-nine years of age and you did promise to me that you would regard seriously the working of our family love spell. This must be considered after the first violets have bloomed then begun fully upon the first day of summer, which will be June 21st. Here are the first violets for you, picked from my own yard. If you have found true love since we last talked, then there is no reason for the spell. If you have not, then please let this help you as it has helped me and your cousin Alma, your own namesake grandmother and my sister Ruby, and so many other women of our relation to find the best mate.

I know you are a modern girl and surely think these things quite foolish, but it has been proven again and again and you are of a family honored to know this secret spell and therefore you should give it a chance.

Have you met your love yet, or are you ready and willing to visit this summer and try this magic?

We would very much like to see you again.

Hopefully yours,

Aunt May Belle

Yes indeed, there was that spooky old Scottish love spell coming back to haunt her, after a fascinating conversation with Aunt May about all the fine matches it had made through the years and how each part of the spell prepared a woman for marriage. How it could bewitch her into finding the right husband, and how this was a well-guarded secret among the women of the family, and how Ruby wasn't getting any younger. She gave Aunt May a few points to her credit for not using scare tactics and mentioning the latter fact again, or for bringing up the dreaded thirtieth year looming next June 17th. Turning thirty would of course automatically make Ruby a dried-up, cardigan-wearing, canary-collecting old maid who smelled like liniment and laundry starch—it would happen like that overnight, along with a head of gray hair and chin whiskers. That was how the rumors went and that was why so many girls got scared into lousy marriages, but at least they weren't thirty and unmarried, because as all the world knew, better a lousy husband than no husband at all.

It was too bad Guzzling Glad hadn't gotten her paws on this communiqué, Ruby thought, because it would have raised her already upwardly penciled-in eyebrows. She would have been about to burst over the idea of magic and spells and hoodoo being conjured up in northeast Pennsylvania, land of coal mines, farms, hills and country folk—and the pocket of the world where Ruby's father's family came from, specifically a town called Bright Bend. Though Ruby's father had law-booked himself into a successful career in Philadelphia and had raised his daughter as a city girl, filling her mind with such independent thought that Ruby didn't even really care about being on the cusp of thirty and chin whiskers.

She therefore decided to wait another year to try the spell, if she tried it at all. Ruby was a little leery toward love and romance anyway, just because her father had been so sadly consumed with feelings for her mother, who had been unworthy of any feeling except disgust. But you could never convince him of that, despite all his logic and braininess and sharp-wittedness otherwise—he had always had a blind, helpless obsession toward her mother and let her use him shamelessly.

Ruby did not want to be either a user or used, and being slender, pretty and clever with dark wavy hair and light brown eyes, she had found it easy enough to meet and date and not get too entangled in seriousness. She also tended to attract men who did not wish to be entangled themselves, and therefore things worked out fairly harmoniously. Although her present beau was something of a puzzler, claiming to not be looking for a wife yet expecting Ruby to be wife-like. With increasing attendance at family parties, where she had to sit and roll her eyes and listen to hints about upcoming weddings and advice about how to give Pete the push to finally settle down.

Pete was a dishy black-haired piano player, and while his nose might have been a whit too sharp, he had dreamy bedroom eyes and a mouth like Rudolph Valentino. He went by the stage name Pete Nickels and played with the dance band Sunny Bill and His Moonbeams, though in truth he had been born Pete Niccolini in South Philadelphia only ten blocks from where Ruby lived now. Pete still resided with his family, where as the handsome and talented only son in the middle of four daughters, he was ridiculously pampered by his mother and pretty much expected to be pampered for the rest of his days.

Pete and Ruby had been hanging around for about five years, four and a half of them intimate. Before even meeting Pete, Ruby had already "crossed the border" as some girls said—actually, she had crossed it twice since blithely losing her virginity—and she crossed it with Pete because he was fun and funny and she had known he'd be an excitable lover. And that was all fine and enjoyable, but he did drive her somewhat batty every now and then. He had trouble arriving on time and in general kept an erratic schedule; he was a musician and most of them were skirt-chasers; and he had also been downright spoiled by his mother's homemade ravioli and fig cookies and her tender, careful hand-washing and ironing of all of Pete's shirts.

Furthermore, for every time that Pete told Ruby that he did not want to get married and she shouldn't try to "cage" him, he would later state that *she* should want to marry him and bear his children. He also wasn't thrilled about Ruby's job, as the assistant to the editor of *Leisurely and Lively Ladies* magazine, and how it took up so much of her thought and energy and had her working in town wearing snazzy dresses and hats and "sauntering" (Pete's word) around with city types. Never mind that Pete was on stage or on the road every weekend at dances or in clubs, with less than wholesome women eyeing him from the audience or while they bounced from table to table hawking cigarettes. Or never mind the fact that there was talk about the band's leaving Philadelphia permanently for New York, with no mention of Ruby in those plans. Pete simply wanted to tell her what was what, and to have her waiting in the wings or not waiting in the wings—or waiting in her apartment like she was now.

Ruby and Pete had agreed to celebrate her birthday a few days late, because Pete had known he would traveling with Sunny Bill on the exact date and had already slipped her a fringed silk shawl for her present. He always gave tiptop birthday and Christmas presents, or incidental gifts because he had seen something in a store window that caught his eye, but he was also frequently broke and tended to drink much of his salary or lose it in card games. Such was Pete. And Pete was currently late by about an hour, which was no major catastrophe and to be expected. Still, as the clock edged its way around another hour of lateness and Ruby sat in the sunset dusk of the day before the longest day of the year, she started to have strange sensations.

She felt stirred by the breeze coming through the window by the fire escape; she felt restless and bored with waiting once again for Pete's arrival; and she kept eyeing the letter from her Aunt May, the envelope of which was beginning to glow weirdly in the half-light. Because she hadn't turned the living room lamp on, of course, and because it was dusk and because she was curious about that spell. Did it really work? Could it really work? Her cousin Alma had done the spell, and Alma now had the sweetest funniest husband

and the two of them still laughed like teenagers even after nearly twenty years together. Aunt May had done it and had had a happy marriage to Uncle Zerah, and apparently there had been other well-wed women in their family including Ruby's own grandmother who had gone through this rigamarole. She wondered what her father would think. He had been quite the sarcastic skeptic on many subjects, but then he had also been a secret romantic and loyal to his upstate hometown and his family's quirky customs.

She pondered the whole idea further, drumming her fingers on a brown velvet pillow on the couch. She had just quit her *Leisurely and Lively Ladies* job and though she had offers for work at other magazines, she hadn't accepted any yet. Ruby had left the job not because of Pete's disapproval, but because her longtime boss had been removed of his duties. Her boss was Mr. Plumwood, a Philadelphia blueblood who owned the publishing conglomerate that featured *Leisurely and Lively Ladies* among its titles.

Mr. Plumwood's family had backed the magazine venture because their scion had a way with words and needed something to do. The family had wanted to compete with Curtis Publishing's impressive empire just a few blocks away in Washington Square, but they were nowhere as successful. Mr. Plumwood binged too much. He went for martinis, cocaine, girls and boys— Plumwood was all over the map, but he and Ruby had always gotten along well. She had handled much of the running of *Leisurely and Lively Ladies* and gently but firmly nudged away Mr. Plumwood's occasional advances, but he'd contracted something serious now like cirrhosis or syphilis—or both—and needed to spend a good while at a clinic. The official story was that his nerves were shot and he was heading off for an extended rest and plenty of Arizona sunshine, but Ruby knew otherwise. Unfortunately, Mr. Plumwood's sister was taking the helm and she was a snippy shrew who had demoted Ruby to a mere typist, so Ruby had duly typed I QUIT onto a piece of paper, left it in the roller and otherwise exited the scene.

Beyond that drama, Mr. Plumwood had given Ruby an excellent severance package, while her father's will had made Ruby heir to a thousand dollars and her father's boyhood home up in Bright Bend, so she wasn't too strapped for cash. The boyhood home was just a wooden box house built around 1880, but it had an acre of land and possibilities, and summer nights in the mountains were cooler than they could ever be in Philadelphia. Ruby wasn't keen on spending another summer in the city, especially in this top floor apartment where all the street soot and heat from outside drifted upward in a thick haze that practically bent the blades of the electric fan. She could take a short vacation, see what the spell nonsense was about, fix the house up, plant vegetables and breathe some cleaner air. And while she had of course been miserable about her father's death and funeral, she had enjoyed seeing Aunt

May and Alma again after so many years and to be able to hang around with them and conjure up men would surely be a treat.

"What to do," she wondered out loud now, still fretting her fingers against the sofa pillow. Then she suddenly decided to make a bet with the cosmic workings of life, and she said that if Pete had not shown up by nine-thirty, she would head for Bright Bend and try the love spell. If he did show up by nine-thirty, she would enjoy her belated birthday party and opt for trying the spell on June 21st of 1930. At age *thirty*: thirty being the major lucky or unlucky number here. She was more in the mood for champagne, cake and silliness tonight and was personally rooting for next year's option, but she also knew you had to stick with a cosmic bet once you'd made it and that if she did have to leave soon, she'd better start packing.

She threw some slips and underwear and dresses into her suitcase, then grabbed an empty hatbox and tossed soaps and creams and a hairbrush into that. The last train to get her there departed at ten-thirty p.m., and if she left promptly at nine-thirty and caught a cab, she should have no trouble making it to the station in time. If she happened to meet Pete at any point upon departure, then that would require turning back and spending half an hour listening to his barrage of questions about just where the hell she did she think she was going on a night they had a date. But there was no sign of Pete. Nine-ten became nine-twenty, then nine-thirty arrived. Ruby hesitated for a moment, then went to the typewriter she kept on her desk to write letters and while she didn't peck out I QUIT, she did type the following words:

> GLADYS,
>
> HAD TO GO SEE MY RELATIVES UPSTATE AND ATTEND TO AN URGENT FAMILY MATTER. WILL BE IN TOUCH SOON AND WILL ALSO SEND THE RENT CHECKS, SO PLEASE KEEP MY APARTMENT FOR ME. PLEASE ALSO FEED RAGBAG IF SHE IS AROUND.
>
> THANK YOU!
>
> RUBY PRITCHARD

Gladys was such a snoop that she'd open the door for Pete when he eventually showed up and see the note right away. Pete would be perplexed and angry, but then again he shouldn't keep a girl waiting two and a half hours for her birthday party. On top of many other tardy arrivals through the years, since Pete only seemed capable of punctuality when he had to be at a show and play the piano—then he managed to find and use his watch. And Ragbag was a fat calico that came up the fire escape once a week to torment pigeons or beg for a bowl of cream, but Ragbag clearly was mooching off of many kind souls and would survive without Ruby.

Gladys had her door open on the first floor and was blaring the Victrola; her apartment was like her dressing room had once been, full of flowers and framed clippings and photographs of her former Glad Glory. She had the music on so loud that she didn't see Ruby slip by or even catch her slinking into a taxi, which immediately turned north to hurry Ruby toward Reading Terminal and an unexpectedly Appalachian summer.

While Ruby was in the cab, she realized that not everyone kept late hours in Bright Bend and that her unannounced after-midnight arrival might cause some disturbed slumber. She had just enough time before boarding to scratch out a telegram to her cousin Alma and send it from Philadelphia, with confident knowledge that everybody in Bright Bend did fuss over everyone else's business and that the station agent there would read the wire and have it immediately delivered to Alma. And sure enough, when the train chugged into the bend that was not so bright at the moment because it was two a.m., Alma was there yawning and waiting. She perked up when she saw Ruby step down onto the platform and hurried over to give her a hug.

"I can't believe you're here and you're going to try our spell!" she exclaimed. "This will be a real adventure, I'm sure. Mom doesn't know yet but she'll be thrilled to the gills when she finds out. Now let's scramble back to my house and get to bed, because duty calls and Jasper and I have to get up early tomorrow to open the store."

Alma and Jasper ran the Bright Bend pharmacy, a wonderful place full of cures and ointments, cosmetics, perfumes, soaps, cigars, cigarettes, pipe and chewing tobacco, as well as magazines, candy, ice cream and fountain drinks. Alma was Aunt May's youngest child and Ruby's second cousin; she was slim, smart and talkative, with lovely blue eyes that she indifferently hid behind oval wire-rimmed glasses. Alma's husband Jasper was also slim, smart and talkative, sporting a tidy moustache and a bespectacled precise manner—but his sense of humor was sharp and even occasionally wicked and he and Alma were always cracking jokes together. Jasper was a love spell groom, and after almost two decades of Jasper and Alma being husband and wife, best friends and business partners, there was no doubt that they had an ideal match.

Alma and Jasper's house was the most modern home in town, newly built to their specifications, with a telephone, all the latest plumbing, and a garage—a structure that no one else in Bright Bend had yet. While more people there had cars now in 1929 then they'd had even five years ago, they parked them out on the street or even occasionally on the front or back lawn. But Jasper was once again leading Bright Bend forward with his newfangled garage that had a cement floor and space for his tools and lawn mower, along with another nook for Alma's gardening things.

The Darbys, better known as Alma and Jasper, also had a radio, an electric vacuum cleaner and an icebox that wasn't really an icebox—it was called a refrigerator and kept itself cold with electricity. Ruby even had a bowl of thoroughly chilled fruit salad from the beauteous refrigerator before going to bed in Alma and Jasper's snazzy chartreuse Art Deco motif guestroom. She slept well, eased along by the scent of honeysuckle outside her window and by the hint of walnut oil that Alma used to polish her wood furniture. In fact, she slept so well that when she woke Alma and Jasper had already gone to the pharmacy and left coffee in the percolator and a glass of fresh-squeezed juice in the fridge. Alma had left a note as well:

COME OVER TO THE PHARM WHEN YOU RISE AND SHINE
THEN WE'LL GO SEE MOM AND GET THIS BARREL ROLLING!

Ruby smiled and sipped her coffee, wondering if anyone had found her own note back in Philadelphia. And if so, what had the reaction been: outrage, indifference, or simply good riddance? But then she shouldn't be worrying about that, she figured, because she had packed up, walked out and made her choice, and now it was indeed time to push the barrel forward.

If her daughter Alma's house represented modern times in Bright Bend, Aunt May's trellised cottage was a showcase of the past. Aunt May still happily preferred candles to light bulbs, her outdoor hand pump to indoor faucets, a root cellar to refrigeration, and a woodstove to the natural gas-flamed version. She had allowed the installation of an indoor privy, however, because she was in her seventies now and Bright Bend winters were long and cold. Otherwise she made her home work well and efficiently, grew her own garden, canned fruits and vegetables, cured meat, put up preserves, sewed clothes, quilted, and raised chickens and an itinerant Guernsey cow that was grazing by the creek when Ruby and Alma arrived.

These days Aunt May was a little wearier than she used to be and struggling with arthritis troubles, but she still had more than a trace of her former wraithlike charm. She was delicate-boned but not delicate, had given birth to five children, lost three of them before they were out of the cradle, been married to Uncle Zerah for thirty-nine years until his death in 1914, helped many a Bright Bender with her herbal tonics and cures, and otherwise brought nothing but warm and caring light to the world. Alma had been Aunt May's last baby, and even though mother and daughter were quite different in the way they wanted time's arrow to fly, they shared a good-natured purposefulness and desire to improve whatever situation they happened upon.

When Alma brought Ruby in to Aunt May's always lemony smelling clean-swept place, Aunt May was churning butter in the kitchen, but she jumped up to give her great-niece a hug.

"Is she ready?" she asked Alma.

"She is!" Alma affirmed.

Aunt May was wearing a patchwork dress she had made from paisley and floral fabric scraps and her once-golden now-silvery white hair was wound up in its usual bun. Her blue eyes gleamed and she did a jig.

"I've just never been so tickled," she laughed.

"Me neither," Alma chimed in, but then she excused herself to get back to the pharmacy and said she would catch up with May and Ruby in the evening.

After finishing the butter and pressing a round of it under a special daisy-patterned mold, Aunt May got right to business.

"Here is our spell," she said, speaking in a low and confidential voice and advising Ruby that this was only to be discussed among the female members of the family. Ruby had expected a yellowed scroll covered with spidery writing, but Aunt May had a stack of typed cards instead, this being Alma's handiwork.

"She said she wanted it to be easier to read and that the original parchment was too dusty and made her sneeze," Aunt May sighed. "Alma can't stand any of the old traditions. I was surely there when she came out of me, but otherwise I'd never believe she was my child. Now I'll keep all the steps of the spell here, so you don't start doing things out of order or reading ahead. And the rule is, you don't have to go through all the steps but you do have to keep going until love finds you. Alma found Jasper at the beginning of her summer spell, while it took me a few more steps into the process. I know what you have to do to start it all tonight, but let's get you settled in your own little house and you can begin from there."

"My own little house?" Ruby repeated. "You mean Dad's old place?"

Her father's boyhood home had been languishing for years, and even before then had been much like Aunt May's: small and primitive, but without the indoor toilet. Ruby had inherited the house when her father had died, but she hardly thought it was livable.

"Oh, we gussied it up for you," Aunt May insisted, and she took her straw hat off a hook on the back of the door and told Ruby that they'd stop in town for some things, then head on over. In town, Aunt May introduced Ruby to a pack of people, including the train station agent, the grocer and hardware store owner (these were the same person), and some fellow Baptists. The post office was pointed out, once having been a stop on the Underground Railroad. There was portly postmistress Hazel as well, who seemed to believe that Ruby's father had been in love with her back around 1893 but had been too shy to speak up.

"He wasn't shy and he wasn't in love with her," Aunt May explained later. "And he used to call her Hazel-*nut*, because she was full of crazy ideas like that."

At the grocery store Aunt May purchased cornmeal, buttermilk and bread, along with various other basic foodstuff items for Ruby's pantry. Normally Aunt May soured her own buttermilk, baked her own bread and gathered eggs from her six hens, but she had just enough for herself and maybe a bit of company and it was easier to buy Ruby her own.

It was getting hot even for June and a heady wind wound its way up Main Street, making some of the shop signs creak and swing on their chains. Aunt May paused to pat at her heart-shaped face with a handkerchief dabbed in rosewater.

"I just want to tell you that you might start to feel things differently," she murmured in the same secret voice as she had when initially discussing the spell. "Once you begin what you're going to begin tonight. Also things can happen quickly and all in a rush. You may find yourself swept away."

Ruby listened politely, but she was observing the midday laziness of Bright Bend and the mutt dog sprawled at the entrance of the grocery store, hoping for bones, while the town shoemaker and tailor brought a chair onto the sidewalk, then spent several minutes adjusting it by half-inches to catch the maximum breeze. Then he just stared straight ahead while a little boy dragged a stick along the sidewalk, and outside Alma and Jasper's pharmacy a bird-like woman paused to consult her shopping list, reading the items aloud while moving her lips. It didn't seem possible that there could be any sweeping away or excitement in a town like this, but perhaps Aunt May knew better.

They continued on to Ruby's new home, which Ruby almost didn't recognize when she saw it. Though the box of a house was still on a rocky and rutted dirt road, it had been repainted and re-roofed; there were gleaming red shutters and a red front door, morning glories twisting up on stakes and a patch of tiger lilies by the entrance. Inside Ruby found new flooring, clean white walls, a new stove and icebox and even new plumbing, including a pearly smooth clawfoot tub. There was a slightly used yet newly covered couch, a cherrywood table and trio of almost-matching chairs, scatter rugs, and not just one tiny furnished bedroom but two, including sheets and pillows and cedar chips to keep moths out of the closets. The kitchen had pots and pans, the cupboard had dishes and flatware and cups and saucers; there was a billowing green fern in the front room and a potted sprig of ivy in the kitchen, everything so fairy-tale like that Ruby literally felt her mouth dropping open.

"Alma and Jasper and I put our heads together to make this a better roost," Aunt May elaborated. "We found furniture here and there, and I knew some nice fellows looking to earn a few dollars carpentering and painting, and Alma's always willing to get rid of her old dishes and pans so she can buy new ones. And before you say a word about paying us back, your father came to Jasper's aid a couple of years ago when a lady tried to accuse him of killing her husband with the wrong medicine. She was pulling a number on everyone and could have ruined Jasper's reputation, but your father cut her and her story down to mincemeat. We all owed him so much, and we want you to spend more time up here. And Alma insisted on having lots of colors because she said when she visited you in Philadelphia your apartment was bright as a jewel box. Careful!" she warned, holding Ruby by the belt of her dress, since Ruby was about to step through the kitchen door onto a back porch that didn't exist yet. "We weren't able to finish that in time, and the wood was too rotted through to save. So use the front door for now," she advised. "I'll get Ben Greenlee to take care of it. Ben might also be your love spell gentleman but we'll have to let that come to pass on its own, won't we?" she smiled.

"We could," Ruby said uncertainly, not wanting to commit to any love spell gentleman she hadn't met yet. "And Aunt May, if ever I understood the phrase from the bottom of my heart, it's now, because you and Alma and Jasper have gone way beyond what ever was expected. I love this place! I have to confess, I was dreading even setting foot in it before."

"It was never the same after your Grandma Ruby died," Aunt May agreed. "She was the soul of the house. Then your Grandpa Luke passed away and your father never visited much and it just faded. But now we'll watch it bloom again, with our new Ruby."

Tomatoes were earlier than usual this year so Aunt May was able to christen Ruby's stove by frying up some green ones breaded in the cornmeal and buttermilk they'd just purchased. They made sandwiches from them and ate them along with iced raspberry tea, a beverage that was also helpful during ladies' days, Aunt May noted.

"Raspberries and their leaves tone the womb," she detailed. "I try to get Alma to drink it more often because I think it'll help her conceive and hold a child, but she's not partial to the idea. She's had three miscarriages and I think she wants to give up. She says she's thirty-eight and getting too old for pregnancy, but I was just about her age when she was born and I've known women who've gone into labor the very same day that their eldest daughter was getting married. Until a woman's in her middle forties, the joyous surprise of a baby is always possible."

While Aunt May had been talking, Ruby had glimpsed a stooped-over man in grimy long johns scurrying past a rain trough toward what appeared to be an outhouse. Fortunately his commode and ramshackle home were far away enough from Ruby's that if she just kept the kitchen curtains shut, she wouldn't have to regularly witness this unsavory routine while she was eating or cooking.

"That's Henry Gwynn," Aunt May said. "I knew him years ago and we went to school together, and to a barn dance or two. I did my share of courting but I always had a feeling I'd end up with your Great Uncle Zerah, even when he decided he wanted to roam and took off to Canada for a year. Henry was married too but his wife passed away and he's turned strange with time. Barely eats and just drinks bottles of Kilmer Swamp Root Tonic, won't speak to anyone and lives in that awful old shack muttering to himself. He won't bother you much, though. He's harmless."

Ruby then heard a muffled ringing sound, or the miraculously progressive inclusion of a telephone in her home. It had been hooked up in one of the closets for some reason, but it still existed and Ruby assumed correctly that Alma had been the one to suggest that feature. It was Alma on the phone now, not surprisingly. She said that her older brother and Aunt May's only surviving son James had sent a package of treats from St. Louis, where he practiced as an architect, along with pictures of Aunt May's granddaughter's high school graduation. And that somebody had found a scrawny orange kitten abandoned down by the lumberyard, and since Aunt May had a soft spot for orange kittens, she jumped up out of her chair.

"Be there in a flash!" Aunt May called, shouting so loudly that even Henry Gwynn turned around, startled, on his way back from outhousing. "Ruby, Alma and I will see you later, but for now you need to stitch yourself a pouch about the size of an envelope from these satin scraps and thread I brought. Can you sew, dear? I know your mother wasn't fond of sewing or cooking or housework, so you may never have learned."

"I learned," Ruby said. "We had a housekeeper named Agnes for years, and Aggie taught me to cook and sew and clean. It was always fun to hang around the kitchen with her. Then we had another housekeeper named Sophie, and she taught me how to cook even better and use all sorts of herbs and spices. She also taught me more French than my French teacher ever could. In fact, why don't you and Alma come over here for dinner tonight? I've got what I need to make potato and onion crepes, and if you bring some kind of vegetable from your garden and Alma brings dessert, we've got a meal. And I'd say that tarragon would be best for the crepe filling tonight. I brought my spice box along with me, of course."

Ruby had her hair pulled into a loose knot and Aunt May tugged playfully at a wisp that had worked its way free.

"Here I thought you wouldn't even be able to thread a needle and you're talking about spices and making fancy crepes," she chuckled. "Which I've never had but they're just real flimsy pancakes, right?"

"I would say that describes them quite well," Ruby agreed.

"Then I would say that I'll have a plate of them for sure," Aunt May replied.

After Aunt May had left, Ruby unpacked her suitcase and poked around her new old home, then she set to work on stitching up the satin pouch she was supposed to use for the beginning of the spell. She sat on the sofa with her legs tucked under her, sewing and thinking about her father growing up in this same place. He hadn't been born in the house but had moved in with his parents as a boy, then had come of age in Bright Bend, fished, teased girls, read every book he could get his hands on, studied by the woodstove, won a scholarship to the University of Pennsylvania and stayed there through law school.

At that point, Andrew Jarvis Pritchard had been thin and resilient as a reed, looking poetic and pale and romantic but tending more towards zinging humor and sarcasm. He should have ended up as a respected judge, but he chose the wrong wife and never quite reached his potential. Ruby's mother had been working in a Chestnut Street flower shop when they'd met, and while she was stunning, she'd had low morals and high ambitions. Her name was Elizabeth but she insisted on being called Isabel; she had come from a no-nonsense middle class family that didn't appreciate her brunette glory and so she cut them all out of her life.

Isabel had had her eye on Andrew Pritchard's best friend, a wealthier law student who bought many flowers for his many girlfriends, but she sensed that she wouldn't be able to control him as easily as she could Andrew, so she married Andrew then had an affair later with the friend instead. She spent money that Andrew didn't have by ordering expensive dresses and hats and wanting to be taken to restaurants and the theater; she also wanted a live-in housekeeper, especially after Ruby was born. She had almost nothing to do with Ruby and let the help or her husband handle all that, and Ruby's only memory of physical contact with her mother was a time that Isabel had slapped her full force in the face for knocking over a bottle of perfume on Isabel's dressing table.

Isabel had not wanted to name her daughter Ruby after Andrew's mother and had complained that the name was too hillbilly-ish, but then she had changed her mind and said that it would be fine as long as Andrew gave her a pair of teardrop ruby earrings to reward her generosity. Andrew couldn't afford the earrings either, but he simply added them to the list of other things that were driving him into debt. To bring those debts down, he accepted a job at an esteemed firm that handled the cases of rich Philadelphians like Ruby's magazine boss Mr. Plumwood. The salary was high, but her father had had to compromise his talents and scruples to essentially handle various family scandals and shady business matters. Ruby went to boarding school in Maryland until she was about fifteen, and while she and her father wrote frequent silly and affectionate letters to each other, she didn't hear from or miss her mother at all.

Her mother had other flings and drained even more life out of her father, and then Isabel announced that she was having nervous problems that could only be cured by a Dr. Abernathy, who had a health resort in North Carolina. And that she would have to "take residence" at that resort in order to be cured. Her father paid those bills too while Ruby's mother had an affair with Dr. Abernathy, though Dr. Abernathy did more bedside work than Ruby's mother was aware of. She caught him in the act with another bosomy naked patient and in a fit of shock and jealousy, Isabel faked a suicide attempt with some sedatives to make Dr. Abernathy feel guilty and to bring him back to her side. The only problem there was that she'd mismeasured doses and unintentionally succeeded in dying, her last reported words being "Goddamn bastard—didn't really want to kill myself over him."

While Ruby considered life infinitely better without Isabel scheming and sashaying around, her father sunk into a grim depression. He began to smoke too much and neglect his health, and he was either pining over past illusions of Ruby's mother or blaming himself for not making her happy enough while she was alive. You could never reach him on that subject; he was just fractured where Isabel was concerned. They did move out of their larger, costlier house to a cozy place on Hicks Street, which Ruby loved, like she also loved trying to tempt her father's appetite with special meals, emptying his heaping ashtrays and opening windows and letting fresh air and sunshine into his study every now and then. He accepted a position at a different firm and was handling the challenging cases he should have taken on earlier, and he taught law at Temple University and enjoyed that very much. He wouldn't remarry, however, or even think about other women, and he worked too hard, almost trying to make up for lost time.

Ruby eventually moved to her own apartment to allow for a bit more independence, but she was still only just blocks away and made sure to keep coming over to cook and toss cigarette butts and challenge her father into exasperated conversations. Her father wanted her to study and become a writer or professor of literature, whereas Ruby preferred a more haphazard path. He also disliked her choice in boyfriends—notably piano-playing Pete—but he did seem proud of his daughter's integrity and willingness to support herself, these qualities ironically making her the complete opposite of her mother.

When her father had his first stroke last spring, she had hoped he might recover and that she could bring him back to Bright Bend for a while at least, so that he could be in a place that he loved and doted over by Aunt May and Alma. But he'd had a second stroke soon after and never regained consciousness, and thus Andrew J. Pritchard died at the too-young age of fifty-four. He had looked much older, though, and at the time of his death his hair was completely white. Ruby accompanied the body to Bright Bend so that he could be buried in the family plot. Her mother had been buried in a Philadelphia cemetery and her father had been visiting her grave weekly with a bouquet of tea roses, but Ruby did not want this strange final closeness to continue on anymore or for her mother to be anywhere near her father in death.

All the recollections of Andrew J. had made the pouch-stitching go fast, and Ruby was tying her final knots and rewinding thread spools soon enough. Despite the sad memories, Ruby had to laugh at a story Alma had told her this morning, about how Ruby's mother had made just one trip to Bright Bend, and not too willingly either. Isabel had still been harping on Andrew's hill people roots and Andrew had been so eager for her to like his family that he had asked that they try to act as sophisticated as possible, for Isabel's sake. Aunt May had gotten huffy over that comment and had encouraged her son James, then sixteen, and Alma, then seven, to meet Andrew and Isabel at the train station dressed in rags and overalls and sunbonnets like "hill people," and to bring along Aunt May's favorite goat Jehoshaphat. Isabel had been disgusted, Andrew J. had laughed hard in spite of that disgust, and while Ruby was just a bun in the oven then—as Aunt May had put it—she was glad to have been there in some form and hoped she had kicked her mother plenty from within while she'd had the chance.

Close to six that night, Ruby was surprised to see Alma's husband Jasper drive up to the house, hauling in himself, Alma, Aunt May, a sewing machine, a dressmaker's form and a bicycle. Everything and everyone made its way out of his car, though a few minutes later Jasper jumped back in.

"He's going to a local business league gathering," Alma detailed. "That's where they discuss business matters for half an hour then drink beer and look at naughty pictures for the rest of the meeting."

Jasper winked. "Yes, we do—and I think I saw Ruby in one of those naughty flipbooks last time we all convened," he said. Ruby shook her fist at him and he drove off, waving.

Aunt May fortunately hadn't heard this racy exchange and was busy dragging the sewing machine and dressmaker's form into Ruby's spare bedroom.

"You ought to have these, honey," she said. "Alma and Jasper bought me them for my birthday and I appreciate the notion dearly, but I still prefer my old treadle machine and wooden dressmaker's frame."

"We were hoping to lure her into getting electricity in her home through the excitement of an electrified sewing machine," Alma added. "But no dice. She's a diehard foot pedal pusher, which is why she still has such nice gams."

Aunt May lifted her skirt to display her legs and Ruby whistled.

"What about the bicycle?" Ruby asked. "Is that Aunt May's too and another reason why she has such nice gams?"

"No, Tim Finn was selling that earlier today," Alma said. "He's moving up to a motorcycle now that he's seventeen and planning to become our local motorcycle cop. Whether the Sheriff agrees with the idea or not, Tim's just going to ride around and write out tickets and all. But since you won't have a car, Ruby, you might want a bicycle for going in and out of town."

"Honestly, I never knew a bunch of inbred hillbillies could be so generous," Ruby said, and Alma shrieked that if this daughter was going to turn into her snooty mother she should be fed to the pigs.

It turned out that Alma and May had brought pajamas and nightgowns, respectively, and intended to sleep over.

"It's your first night in the house and it might be nice to have company," Alma said. "And that way we can all be here for the start of the love spell."

"And we can stand for three different phases of the spell," Aunt May noted. "Past, present and future."

Ruby had made her crepes and Aunt May mixed a salad of wild greens and scallions, and Alma had bought a lemon meringue pie from Mrs. Miller's boardinghouse dining room, which was considered the best place to eat in town outside of your own kitchen. The crepes and salad were pronounced delicious, and the eating of the pie gave Alma and May the chance to do what most pie-baking women greatly enjoy—finding fault with a commercially sold product.

"This meringue has an oiliness," Alma complained. "And the filling's too sweet."

"There's no matching Mary Miller's crust, though. Flaky through and through," Aunt May said, and even Alma had to admit to that.

When the sun finally set on the solstice, it was Ruby's job to find the largest pinecone she could out in the nearby woods. She avoided going too close to Henry Gwynn's outhouse and hunted around, got startled by a bat or two then hurried back inside with her choice.

"That's a grand one," Aunt May praised. "So you'll put this into the pouch you sewed earlier, then slip the pouch and the pinecone under your pillow and be sure to remember what you dream, because it will foretell your true love."

"I dreamed about a pocket watch," Alma recalled, smiling. "Then two days later I was going to the pharmacy to buy Mother some peppermint oil and there was a young man standing outside the door looking at—guess what? His pocket watch. He was our pal Jasper, just getting here to start as our new town pharmacist. I only married him because he had that watch, of course," Alma joked. "Good thing he wasn't an axe murderer. Though he would have been punctual, I guess."

"I had a dream about light blue silk," Aunt May said, smiling now also. "Bolts and bolts of it, spilling out everywhere. So when Alma's father and your Great Uncle Zerah came back from Canada, he'd brought me a blue silk pillow with beaded trim, because he said the blue of it had reminded him of my eyes."

"Good Lord!" Ruby burst out. "What if I don't dream anything? Sometimes it's just a blank movie screen all night. Will I get another chance?"

"You'll dream of something, don't worry," Alma said assuredly, though Ruby remained unconvinced.

As official bedtime approached, Ruby grew even more anxious, and when she slowly slid the pinecone into the satin pouch she wondered if she was the only one to notice how sexual the whole thing was. Pinecone, pouch, insertion—all classic Freudian stuff. She worried too that her not being intact and virginal might cause the spell to fail, because Aunt May and Alma had no doubt been chaste at the time of their conjuring. Ruby was of a different generation and had been of an inquisitive mindset since her late teens, and she had indeed been inquisitive with Pete, one of her father's law clerks, and a well-known actor between performances and marriages.

Her father had suspected the liaisons with both the clerk and with Pete, and he would have been horrified by the actor's appearance, though Ruby had found the whole event delightfully detached and fun. The actor had Philadelphia ties and was then in Rittenhouse Square savoring a cigarette after what looked like a long and merry night, just when Ruby had sat on a nearby bench trying to fix the broken heel of her shoe. A casual conversation turned into an encounter; she went along because she was very close to nineteen, curious about such matters, and she happened to be a fan of this particular gentleman. Out of respect for her father, though, she had never spoken of the incident to anyone and she doubted that the actor even remembered it among his many adventures. Ruby, however, would always recall her first matinee and encore fondly and was also appreciative to her shoe heel for waiting for that specific moment to fall off.

"My, don't you look fretful," Aunt May sighed, now standing in the doorway of Ruby's bedroom with her hair twisted into rag curlers. "Don't worry about it so much, dear. Relax and let your dreams tell their own story."

"Sure thing, Rubykins!" Alma called from the couch where she was stretched out in a pair of Jasper's pajamas reading *The Saturday Evening Post*. "Just go to sleep like you've done for every other night of your life."

Ruby nonetheless had insomnia for a while. She stared at the Burpee seed cover catalogs that Aunt May had framed and put in this bedroom, bright beautiful illustrations of sweet peas and zinnias, and then she also noted a botanical print of violets, like the violets Aunt May had sent along with her letter asking Ruby to give this summer's magic a try. She listened to spring peepers and the ticking of her alarm clock, and while she loved everything in this little house, she found the creaking of the bedsprings ridiculously loud. Yet then she did fall asleep and had a dream as promised, and in the dream she was simply walking toward this newfound house reaching for the red door when she saw a shimmering dragonfly with wings like stained glass. So when she woke, she assumed that her symbol was either the dragonfly or the glossy red door, but when she went to ask Aunt May for clarification, Aunt May said not to tell her any details.

"You're supposed to keep it secret," she cautioned. "You can talk about it later but while you're waiting for the dream to come true, it's best to keep quiet. Like setting a lid on a pot to make it boil faster."

Alma had left early for the pharmacy as always and Aunt May needed to tend to her hens and cow, but before she left too she and Ruby had coffee and fried eggs and johnny cakes. Aunt May mentioned Ben Greenlee, the carpenter, beekeeper and apparent moonshiner she had brought up yesterday, though Aunt May insisted that Ben made spirits mostly for medicinal or celebratory purposes and wasn't a lowdown Prohibition-defying hootch peddler.

The more Ruby heard about Ben, the more she had a feeling that she'd already met him when she had come to Bright Bend as a girl. Ruby had made a few trips with just her father, and on one of them there had been a whooping and hollering reunion of sorts in what was called Settlers' Field, with tents set up and fiddling and dancing and drinking and kids and dogs running everywhere.   Ruby had snuck over to investigate the sights and sounds and had been ambushed from behind by a tall black-haired boy who'd tried to flip up her skirt, and who had then laughed and joined the fray. Ruby didn't want to accuse anyone of such wrongdoing until she had more proof, though, so like the dragonfly of her dream and her dicey romantic past, she kept the skirt-flipping attempt quiet.

When Aunt May had gone too, Ruby went to sit on the front porch and contemplate the coming day and how radically her life had changed in two short days. She stretched out her bare legs and also contemplated painting her toenails red to match her glossy door, and to her surprise she thought she saw a dragonfly dart past. Already a dragonfly, but what could it mean since there was no one else around? The dragonfly transformed into a hummingbird, however, whirring near the tiger lilies, and that reminded Ruby of how her father used to tease her about bustling about and cleaning too much and hovering around him like a ruby-throated hummingbird. She smiled and listened to the flurry of the hummingbird's wings as it bobbed up and down and went at the flowers. It wasn't a dragonfly, but that was fine; it seemed more like a personal welcoming symbol from her father, and a sign that for once he might truly think she was doing the right thing.

For sweetness of speech, a spoonful of honey each morn for three morns will help find your truest love.

II.

⚜

Following the mysterious Dream of the Pinecone, Ruby began her love spell venture with a required spoonful of honey first thing in the morning for three straight mornings. This was to encourage sweetness of speech, which every woman evidently needed to soothe and charm her way to—and through—a happy marriage. It irked Ruby, however, that right off she should have to get herself some honey when Aunt May clearly was pushing this beekeeper as Ruby's potential spell mate. So just to have impartial honey involved, Ruby made a point of taking the train two stops north to Royal Bend, which was like Bright Bend's older and more cosmopolitan brother. Royal Bend had a movie theater and an ice cream parlor run by a Greek family, where they served fantastic concoctions such as pistachio ice cream and hot fudge sauce under clouds of whipped cream, and surprisingly the movies shown at the theater were only about six months behind the ones in Philadelphia or New York.

Royal Bend had a wider selection in their grocery store and a bustling farmer's market from summer through fall, and it was here that Ruby bought a jar of honey from a source other than Ben Greenlee. She also bought fresh nutmeg and cinnamon sticks at the grocery, with baker's chocolate so rich it was black in color and a bag of lemons that looked like they'd just been picked off the tree. She decided to sit through Harold Lloyd's *Speedy* again at the theater and later sampled some almond ice cream at Athena's, two of the best scoops of anything she'd ever consumed in her life. Then she skimmed through the *Royal Bend Register* on the trip home, getting an actual laugh out of its slogan: *Published Weekly Unless The Editor Has Something Better to Do.* She further appreciated one of its recent news snippets:

> Mid-June indeed brought much precipitation to our fair
> town. And they say the rain won't hurt the rhubarb—which
> is good to hear, unless you hate rhubarb.

Royal Bend's *Register* even had a couple of articles and an editorial about how liberated the American woman had become in just the past decade— without being against that liberation. The *Bright Bend Banner* didn't have the same breadth or snappy tone, and was generally a single-pager that came out twice a month and detailed who in Bright Bend had been born, died, gotten married or fallen sick, along with a few inspirational quotes or proverbs and a recipe. The recipe always involved ingredients from Lewis Tyler's general store, since Lewis Tyler put together the *Banner*. Ruby wasn't completely disapproving of the paper, though, since Mr. Tyler had already noted Ruby's arrival in Bright Bend for the summer and described her as Andrew J. Pritchard's "winsome and charming" daughter, which was quite a winsome and charming pair of adjectives.

Jasper met her at the train station back in Bright Bend, ready to grill her with questions about his closest rival: the Royal Bend pharmacy.

"I asked you to stop in there because of course Alma and I can't go in, they'll recognize us and think we're snooping around. Which we would be," he explained. "But I hear they've got a new scale that gives you your fortune and your weight. Is that true?"

"Yes, they do have the scale and according to it I weigh one hundred and sixteen pounds and my fortune says I have a curious smile and a mysterious nature."

"Hmm," Jasper said. "In your case I'd switch that to you have a mysterious smile and a curious nature, but go on. How's their grooming and sundries section? And the coffee and soda fountain area?"

"Their grooming and sundries area is bigger with more of a perfume and soap selection," Ruby advised. "But their clerk was rude, which you and Alma never are, and their coffee and soda fountain section is a joke. They've given up because of that Greek ice cream parlor in town. Hardly anyone even gets coffee or ice cream sodas at the drug store, unless they're ridiculously against immigrants. Oh, and Jasper?" she added, hoping to put his insecurities at rest. "Outside the drug store I saw scads of cigarette butts. Nobody was sweeping them away and it looked downright tawdry. You know that would never happen around here."

"It would certainly *not*," he confirmed. "So we seem to have courtesy, cleanliness, fountain drinks, ice cream and coffee keeping us in the running. Well, that's enough. By the way, Alma asked me to ask you if you'd gotten what you went there for." He grimaced. "Which is no doubt something female-related so don't tell me what it is, just tell me yes or no so I can tell her."

"But Jasper, how can you call yourself a pharmacist and not want to hear about the shaving of legs and eyebrow plucking or monthly ladies' days?" Ruby teased.

"Those belong in Alma's territory," Jasper said. "While I capably handle male flatulence, thinning hair, piles and constipation." He pointed to Ruby's grocery bag. "So is whatever's in your paper sack there what you wanted to have in your paper sack?"

Since the spell was supposedly a womanly family secret, Jasper couldn't be let in on the honey purchase, so Ruby just nodded and said to inform Alma that it had been a successful mission.

Three days of honey mouthfuls passed, and then the following afternoon while Ruby was dozing through her father's edition of *War and Peace* with a glass of iced coffee on the front porch, a lanky presence approached. He was a distinct combination of what looked like an Indian warrior and Abe Lincoln in his rail-splitting days; his dark hair was thick and erratically cut, his mouth seemed solemn yet contemplating a smile at the left corner; he had a strong chin, a stronger nose, and an impressive pair of hazel eyes. He wore patched-over pants, a gingham shirt, scuffed workboots and a brown suede hat. He removed the hat to nod at Ruby, then put it back on.

"Sorry to interrupt your nap, but I pretty much understand—that book was a yawner," he said, indicating Tolstoy. "Do you know who I am?"

"Probably Ben Greenlee?" she guessed.

"Probably true," he concurred. "Your Aunt May's one of my favorite people and she asked me to stop by for a visit and say hello. And maybe start building you a new back porch. I already fixed the front porch and painted the house," he noted proudly. "And the red shutters and door here. Your cousin Alma said you love color."

"I do love color," Ruby agreed. "Especially red, and when I saw this place all repainted and repaired I couldn't believe my eyes. I'd visited when I was a kid and it was a shambles then. And do you know once I came up here when I was about nine, twenty years ago, when your family was having a reunion party in Settlers' Field?"

"We sure were and I was about twelve then myself," he said amiably, though he didn't seem to recall trying to flip up her skirt. Skirt-flipping, however, might have been something he'd done all the time back then.

"Would you like some iced coffee?" she offered, also offering him the other wicker porch chair, which he eased right into. Despite his pioneer era clothing, the man had a definite charisma, Ruby had to admit that much.

"Sure would," he said. "I was just wondering what you were drinking there."

Ruby went to the kitchen, filled another glass with ice and milk and a pinch of cinnamon, then added the rest of the morning's coffee. She gave it to Ben who took a cautious sip at first, then swallowed the rest appreciatively.

"Nice," he praised. "Perks you up and chills you at the same time." He had been looking at her father's copy of *War and Peace* and pointed out the monogrammed bookplate on the inside cover. "Ruby, I was sorry to hear about your loss," he added respectfully. "I remember Mr. Pritchard came to talk to us at school once about studying law and learning and finding out about the world. I was in trouble that day because it was hot and I hadn't worn any shoes on purpose, so the teacher made me sit in the hall, but I could still hear what Mr. Pritchard said and afterward he came out and talked to me alone. He asked me what faraway country I'd like to travel to and I said Japan right off, and a couple weeks later he sent a book all about Japan addressed to me care of the school. I still have that book too and while I might not've made it to Japan yet, I sure made it to Japantown in San Francisco and I almost mailed your father a postcard while I was there."

So he did have a memory for truly important things, Ruby thought, forgiving Ben's skirt-flipping brashness while hoping to keep from crying. Ben seemed to realize that Ruby had gotten a tad shaky and rattled the remaining ice in his glass awkwardly while waiting for her to compose herself.

"Say, I just finished another interesting book," he offered as a distraction. "It's called *The Life of the Bee* by Maurice Maeterlinck. He won the Nobel Prize, and I think he's from France or Belgium or Switzerland or one of those countries. I keep bees myself," Ben added matter-of-factly. "They sure are amazing little buzzers."

He provided some compelling evidence to back up his bee awe, like how the queen controlled the hive and drones served the queen; how the workers were females but not fully developed like the queen; how royal jelly could turn a regular female into a queen and how a colony of bees could live for years. That skunks could sniff out a hive and gobble up the bees like salted peanuts, and that bees definitely chose people they liked and disliked.

"Seems to have something to do with if a person's nervous or just has the wrong smell about them," Ben elaborated. "Then they won't like you. They like me the best and my brother's a close second, but the only time I was ever stung was when a poor bee got caught up in my sleeve and all frantic about being trapped. I didn't hold any grudge, though."

Ruby was still feeling honey-glazed from that morning's dose and sweetly encouraged Ben to talk about his travels. He responded with enthusiasm, speaking of trips to California and Oregon, Wyoming, Colorado, Texas and Mexico. He had a mellow loquaciousness that she found appealing, and having always been fond of dark-haired types, he was as easy for Ruby to look at as to listen to. Even with that pre-1900 pair of sideburns.

Ben himself appeared equally charmed and they parted with plenty of smiles and meaningful glances. He had mentioned working on the back porch and said he would be there in the morning to start on it, and regardless of the fact that Ben was notorious for erratic arrivals when it came to carpentry and painting jobs, he was indeed there the next morning. He had brought a small crock of his own honey for her as well, and it was richer and headier than the jar she had bought in Royal Bend—she couldn't deny that. She mixed some of the honey with butter and crushed walnuts, then spread it onto thick slices of bread and brought some with another glass of iced coffee as a snack for Ben, who had been hammering and sawing for hours.

He ate the honeyed bread, drained the coffee glass then looked at her gravely. Then out of nowhere he moved forward and wrapped her in a kiss that had her reeling and caught up in a rib-locking grip that smelled of honey, castile soap, pipe tobacco and enough virile sweat to make it exciting but not offensive. The kiss surprised her so much that she took it in without a word, picking up the empty plate and glass afterward and returning to the kitchen while Ben picked up his hammer and started pounding at planks again. She stayed in the kitchen to calm down a bit, though she still watched him through the window over the sink while she did the breakfast dishes, thinking how perhaps this was what Aunt May had meant about things speeding up and intensifying. Ben continued to work purposefully for about another twenty minutes or so, then he appeared to be answering the chatter of an angry squirrel in the maple tree, then he just sprawled out under the tree altogether for a nap.

Ruby felt she needed some time to contemplate that whirlwind embrace and decided to walk into town to buy another loaf of bread and a can of salmon for lunch. A can of salmon, cucumbers, onions, and mayonnaise for salmon salad, then she could stop by Aunt May's to pick fresh dill for the garnish. Aunt May was outside under her own large maple trees quilting with her sister-in-law Nellie, whom Aunt May had known even before she'd married Nellie's brother Zerah. The ladies hurried to fold up the quilt when Ruby arrived.

"This is for your wedding!" Nellie said. "Don't look or it'll be bad luck."

"My stars—when am I getting married? Do I have time to change my dress?" Ruby joked, though she had seen flashes of scarlet and violet fabric and was not averse to being given a quilt like that.

"So my dear one," Aunt May asked archly. "Has Ben come by to visit?"

"And is he putting those blooms in your cheeks?" Nellie laughed. "She's blooming, isn't she, May?"

"She has an awfully pretty glow," May confirmed.

"Do you think it might be heat stroke?" Ruby asked, but Nellie and May shook their heads knowingly and told her to go make Ben his lunch, because he was such a fine young man with a hearty appetite.

In an unprecedented record of achievement, Ben had the back porch finished in four more days. Normally he would have taken at least two weeks, with a short lapse wherein he would have utterly abandoned the project to go fishing or wandering off to the nearest town to visit friends or relatives. His motivation now seemed to be that he had asked Ruby to make him supper when he was through, and he had declared that he wanted it to be a special supper and advised her that he planned to wear his Sunday best for the event. Ruby was still finding herself unusually honey-mouthed and increasingly under Ben's sway, though she would not confess that to Aunt May or Alma. But she always watched him while he worked, and while he napped or fought with the same squirrel under the same tree. She even thought in amazement that a dragonfly had landed between his shoulder blades, but it turned out to just be a dragonfly-shaped patch of sweat that had formed on the back of his shirt as he banged nails into submission under the warm noon sun.

Because Ben had mentioned having Italian food in San Francisco and enjoying it very much, Ruby decided to use her former beau Pete's mother's recipes for ravioli, fried zucchini and lemon ice for dessert. Since she had observed Mrs. Niccolini in action and cooked the same meal for Pete herself several times, Ruby made the ravioli dough from flour, eggs, oil and water easily enough, then filled them with farmer's cheese and salt and pepper. She didn't have as many authentic Italian ingredients as she would have liked, but she did have dried basil in her spice stash and two big Mason jars full of lush red tomatoes from Aunt May for the ravioli sauce, along with zucchini (or green squash as it was called in Bright Bend) and onions from Aunt May's garden, cornmeal for the zucchini breading and lemons and sugar for the dessert ice. The ice was the easiest thing to fix, with just water, lemon juice and plenty of sugar mixed up then poured into a metal pan and frozen, then loosened into crystals with a fork, then frozen again until ready to serve.

Ruby was busy preparing everything, and she was also flushed from boiling ravioli water, frying zucchini, tending to bubbling pans full of sauce and sweeping fallen flour off the floor. She was caught off guard when Ben arrived early, dressed in a dark suit with a string tie, his hair combed and parted and his face so clean and well-shaven that he looked five years younger. He carried a chaotic bouquet of wildflowers and two beeswax candles, long amber tapers created jointly by his hives and Ruby's Aunt May.

"I'm sorry to be such a mess," Ruby apologized. "I thought we had settled on seven o'clock for dinner."

"We did, but I was all ready and didn't feel like waiting around at home anymore," Ben said. "And you look awful cute in your apron so don't feel inclined to change to impress me. There's nothing sweeter than a woman in an apron. Well, not every woman," he amended. "But in your case I can't imagine anything better."

Now there was a red flag, Ruby thought, with a man preferring her aproned and at the stove, but then again she did like to cook and this was a cute apron. He bent down and kissed her first on her damp forehead, then on the nose, then on the lips.

"Whatever you're doing in there smells dang good," he approved, glancing toward the kitchen. She touched the slight cleft in his own upper lip, smiling, and he kissed her again then picked her up and swung her back to her dinner preparations.

"Normally I could love you up for hours but I'm real hungry tonight," he explained. "My stomach's about to turn itself inside out it's so empty."

The flowers were placed inside a zinc bucket, since there were so many of them and that was the only vessel that would hold the bunch; the candles were lit, plates laid out and dinner served. It was eaten without conversation, though Ben did make various noises and gestures of approval. When he had spooned up the last of his lemon ice and eaten the mint leaf placed delicately on the side, he tossed his napkin onto the table and leaned back with a grin.

"Damn!" he exclaimed. "Excuse my lingo but that was every bite as good as any Italian food I've had before. Now let me offer you a little after-dinner nip." He produced a flask full of orange cordial that he had presumably made, pouring it into teacups because she had no cordial glasses and watching while she drank. "I'm sure you're not used to spirits but every now and then it's all right to have a taste."

I'm sure I am used to spirits and could drink half that flask, she thought, but once again she kept her tongue docile and demure. They moved to the couch to cuddle and digest, and Ben began toying with her hair.

"Nice to see you haven't gotten a bob like so many other gals," he approved. "You're old-fashioned like your great-aunt. You don't want to go around looking like a man."

"But I only haven't bobbed it because it's so thick and curly," she objected vaguely. "If it were too short it'd puff out like poodle fur. If I keep it longer the weight makes it straighter, but otherwise I'd bob my hair in a heartbeat. Just not to deal with snarls and tangles, or to feel the weight of it in the hot weather."

"Keep it long," he persisted, smiling and distracting her with his thorough and hypnotic massaging of the nape of her neck. "Say, how'd you learn to make Italian food like that anyhow?" he asked after a moment.

Ruby had nearly been lulled into a trance by his fingertips, but she murmured something about Pete's mother and her recipes. Ben straightened up and raised a disapproving eyebrow.

"Oh, yeah? And how long did you pal around with that fellow?" he demanded.

"Five years, more or less," Ruby said.

"Five years!" he repeated unhappily. "I hope you're still pure, because it seems like it'd be awfully tough to hold off any Dago for more than a month."

Over on the table one of the beeswax candles flared and sputtered out, and Ruby also began to lose her dulcet restraint.

"Are you still pure, Ben?" she inquired. "Because it seems like it'd be awfully tough to stay that way for thirty-three whole years."

"I'm not expected to be pure," he explained sternly. "I'm a man. Men are supposed to bring experience and wisdom to their wives. And women are supposed to tame and soothe their men."

My, there are so many big red flags flying in here, Ruby thought. Red flags and warning signs and maybe that's what that loony squirrel outside has been screeching about: *Hey there, sister, stay clear of this numbskull!!*

Ben was scowling now, mulling over these latest developments. He had been so proprietary about the orange cordial and she wanted more, so on impulse she reached over, snatched it from him and poured herself another cup, knocking it back in one gulp.

"I'm rather partial to spirits, Ben," she confided, feeling the warm burn of alcohol trail down her throat and into her body. "And experiences. And I've managed to find some of my own pearls of wisdom, even without a man."

He continued to be silent yet then narrowed his gaze at her and nodded. "I was wondering why you hadn't been married off yet," he assessed. "But now I can see that you're kind of contrary. That's sure to keep you from the altar."

Ruby tried to leap up and away from him then, but he had her blocked with one long arm stretched out like a railroad crossing gate.

"Move," she said curtly. "I want to find some scissors and bob my hair then stuff the rest of it down your throat."

He surprisingly let out a loud laugh until she knocked her elbow into his ribs so that he'd jerk his arm to the side. She ran because he was chasing her at that point, and then they both collapsed onto her bed.

"Oh, get off me," she moaned, because he was pushing all the air out of her with his height and weight and because she couldn't stand the closeness. And because she still wanted to hold him and feel him and open herself up completely, even after his idiotic comments. She hated herself for that, and though she had her arms wound around his back and was urging him on, she began to cry from frustration and begged him to stop. He paused and sat up with a final creak of bedsprings, then gently cradled her cheek.

"Shush, shush and listen here," he soothed. "I never wanted you to think that it was over between us—I was only coming to see how you're more than a spitfire than I'd expected. But I like a girl with fire, and we'll just have to work around our differences. And I know how you want to be pure for *me*, because you cried and asked me to stop. That touched my heart. Now you get some rest and we'll talk about all of this tomorrow. Good night, little Ruby."

He left the bedroom and let himself out, while she lay there thinking how she needed to jump off this mattress immediately, pack her suitcase and run as far as possible from this man. Or from anyone who would call her *little Ruby*, for corn's sake—the sake of the corn being the vernacular of Bright Bend. And if she didn't leave town tonight then she would have to have a detached and final talk with him tomorrow. She'd also have to do all the dinner dishes tomorrow, but for right now it seemed best to simply snuff out the other flickering beeswax candle and head back to bed, with maybe a few lingering thoughts of Ben's strength on top of her. Only a few longing surging thoughts and images, then tomorrow she'd be nothing but common sense and clear-headedness where he was concerned.

It rained the next morning until about noon, and then Ruby saw an honest to goodness rainbow and took that as a lucky sign that she would get over this situation and not to let herself be so easily overwhelmed. She stopped by to see if Aunt May's cellar had flooded, which it tended to do during heavy rains, but when she came round the back door to the kitchen she saw how Ben was there and Aunt May was making him a grilled cheese and bacon sandwich. He raised his glass of ginger beer at Ruby and winked.

He's inescapable, she thought, trying not to make direct depthless hazel eye contact.

"Ben was just telling me about the Italian supper you fixed last night," Aunt May said and Ruby smiled, because like Ben she pronounced it Eye-talian. "He swears it's even better than restaurant food he's had."

"And Ben is so well-traveled," Ruby put in. "So full of experiences and knowledge."

"That I am," Ben shot back. "So you might want to learn a thing or two."

"Do you suppose I could?" Ruby asked blankly. "I might get dizzy from thinking too hard."

"Ruby," Aunt May deflected. "I must say you look pretty as a buttercup in your yellow blouse. Now do you think you might do me a favor?"

"Of course, Aunt May," Ruby offered, much to her later regret.

It was revealed that Ben was playing Joseph in a Sunday School pageant that Aunt May was organizing for the tykes at the church, and that he needed his costume done as soon as possible. Aunt May had planned to sew his many-colored tunic today, but the rain had her rheumatism going and joints aching and she wondered whether Ruby might handle the job instead.

"Here's all the fabric and the illustration we're working from," Aunt May said, handing her a wicker basket full of cloth and a resplendent drawing of the prophetic dreamer and son of Jacob. "You've got your machine at home and Ben will come with you so you can take his measurements and make sure everything fits."

Despite the fact that Ben was involved and this was an obvious ploy to unite them through the Book of Genesis and Singer sewing machines, Ruby readily agreed. The costume was more colorful than complicated, and it would be fun to patch together such lovely fabric and golden trim. They drove back to Ruby's in Ben's truck and began work, and had she only had to make the costume and then hand it over to Ben it would have been a fun project indeed. Ben, however, kept coming up with impractical suggestions or insisting that squares of fabric be switched after they'd already been sewn into place. He also complained that there wasn't enough "give" to the tunic even after he'd said it fit fine before, thus requiring seams to be let out and redone, and he hung over Ruby's shoulder asking why she was taking so long.

He furthermore did not like her own frock-in-progress fitted onto the dressmaker form Aunt May had given her, commenting that it looked too "fast" and low in the neck. Then he yelled like a lunatic upon being pricked with a stray pin and at this juncture Ruby felt a burning need to either take a break or stab him with her sewing shears.   She took the break instead, hoping to avoid jail time.   Ben followed her to the kitchen barefoot and in his brilliant Joseph coat, and Ruby had a very aggravated feeling that the multi-colored rainbow she had glimpsed earlier was a cosmic practical joke.

She splashed cold water onto her face then ran some over her wrists.

"You did this up right, girl," Ben praised, smoothing his costume.   "I'm sure to stop the show.   And it was so hot being bent over that sewing machine for hours, wasn't it?"

"Especially with you hovering over every stitch," she muttered.

"Well, I felt you needed guidance."   He squeezed her waist affectionately. "Marry me," he urged.

The squirrel began barking outside and Ruby waved to it from the kitchen window, signaling that she was indeed getting its messages of warning.

"Is somebody in the yard?" Ben asked, looming over her shoulder again. "And if you won't marry me, let's go take a swim.   We could both stand to cool off, I'm sure."

"Yes to the swim and let me change into my bathing suit," Ruby said, pausing just for a second to snap a stray thread from Joseph's regal purple chest.

On the way to Goose Lake—which ironically had many ducks but no geese—they stopped at Ben's place so that he could show her where he lived and let her take a look at the bees.   She had envisioned more of a shack than a neat and well-built cabin and was most surprised, though from what she had heard, Ben's brother George handled most of the upkeep.   The brother was heavier-set than Ben and less talkative, and wherever he walked a pair of beagles followed.   The inside of the cabin was as tidy as the exterior and utterly livable, but the plank floors were a touch too creaky and the air smelled a touch too much of dog and pipe smoke.   Ben's room had plenty of books, an old bed with a new quilt that looked suspiciously like it had been made by Aunt May, a guitar and a calendar from 1925 displaying an illustration of a Mexican girl with black braids, a coy face and bright dark eyes.

"I've always cottoned to her," Ben explained.   "Her month was Abril, which means April in English.   All their months are pretty close to the English ones, except for Enero, which means January," he added thoughtfully. "Otherwise it's not so tough to speak Spanish.   You know any?"

"No Spanish, only French," Ruby said.

"Don't care for French," Ben dismissed.   "Too snooty and speaking it makes you sound like you've got the croup.   Now you could pass for that calendar girl's paler sister if you grew your hair even longer and braided it.   I'd like that." He snatched up the guitar from behind the bureau and began to play and sing:

> *Mexicali Rose, stop crying,*
> *I'll come back to you some sunny day.*
>
> *Mexicali Rosa no llores por mi,*
> *Pienso que volver un buen día…*

"That's *Mexicali Rose* in both languages," he said, and Ruby applauded because he played well and had a clear rich voice. Ben's brother had poked his head in the door along with one of the dogs, and George finally cracked a smile at Ruby.

"Miss Pritchard, is Ben hurting your ears with that wailing?" he asked.

"No!" Ruby laughed. "I think Ben's good enough to sing on a record."

"You hear that, George?" Ben retorted. "So quit your sniping."

Somewhere in the dense woods were their moonshining stills, which Ben said he ran for purely experimental purposes but his brother preferred to sell his product to half the county.

"If it were just me, we'd never get tracked down by the Feds," Ben said. "George is greedy, though, so he'll attract revenuers and get sent to prison eventually."

"Won't you get sent to prison too?" Ruby asked with renewed concern. Ben was a maddening individual for sure, but she didn't want to ever envision him behind bars.

"Not likely," Ben assured her. "I supply the Sheriff's son with spirits, so he'd put in a word for me. I just give him what he likes and don't take a cent for it. It's what I think of as insurance money."

The bees were another story, swarming around a pair of oaks and near a wooden bee box that Ben had set up, and he approached them all with a metal smoker device so that he could puff up a cloud of gently smoldering burlap fumes and keep the hives calm. He walked through unfazed in his netted hat and gloves, though when Ruby came closer the bees seemed cranky and disoriented so she quickly retreated.

At the lake their swim began peacefully, but then Ben got more aggressive. He scooped her out of the water and held her tight, and with the lack of clothing between them Ruby sensed things might get real close real fast. She had also noted Ben's physical prowess while working on his costume and the fact that he swung more than one hammer. He was so damn difficult to pull away from too, just such a tall strapping boundlessly wet-chested healthy *man* that she wanted to hang from like the rope swing near the lake's inlet.

Fortunately, he was also insane and conflicted and took it upon himself to push her back.

"We shouldn't—no, not now," he decided. "We should start pure and baptize ourselves here, then find a preacher and get married. Not that I'm really a Baptist, I just like some of their ideas and it's always nice to help out your Aunt May in the pageants she puts on. Come on now, though. Give me your hand and let your past sins wash away and commit yourself to me."

"*Shall we ga-therrr, at the riv-errrr...*" he began to sing loudly.

Ruby swam off and began doing a sidestroke until Ben dragged her back by the foot.

"I'm serious!" he yelled. "Why won't you ever do anything I ask?"

"Because I am not a sinner or a Baptist or ready to marry you!" she yelled in return.

"But I am ready to get married!" he insisted. "I've resolved that."

"Well, congratulations!" she laughed, yet then to her surprise he took off like a fury, his long arms and legs churning through the water faster than a boat all the way to the other side of the lake. She waited for him to come back but after a while she couldn't even spot him as a dim and far-off figure on the other shore. She screamed his name and only heard echoes in return. After half an hour she waded out of the water, toweled off and got dressed, toying with the idea of pushing his truck into the lake but figuring she should save her strength for the walk home. Which thankfully wasn't as far as most of the other lakes in the area, though she was cursing Ben most of the way. He drove by looking for her at one point, but she hid behind an embankment of rocks, not wanting to speak to him anymore and hoping that he'd worry that she'd been eaten by a mountain lion.

When she did reach town she stopped in at the pharmacy for a tin roof sundae and a glass of cold and fizzy soda water.

"You look sunburned and disgusted," Alma said. "Let me guess—were you just with Ben Greenlee?"

"He's a jackass," Ruby replied flatly. Alma motioned to an auburn-haired young woman with a baby carriage over by the register talking to Jasper.

"That's Jenny Walsh," Alma said. "She courted Ben about two years ago. She used to run the library before she got married and Mrs. Whist took over. I believe she described Ben as close to a jackass herself—but Jenny's rather genteel and just referred to him as a dunce. Jenny, come here and talk to my cousin Ruby while Jasper and I slobber over your baby."

Jenny's daughter was named Charlotte, though Jasper and Alma never called her that and instead gurgled and cooed things like porkpie and dumpling, pigler, jelly bean, gum drop and chickadee. Jenny had the serene weariness of a new mother but seemed glad to meet Ruby and take a break from babyland while sipping a Coke.

"I don't want to badmouth Ben," Jenny sighed. "He's such a smart and unusual fellow—he used to visit the library all the time, that's how we met. And we only were an item for a couple of weeks. That's Ben's problem, he's only got about a week's worth of charm in him before he starts showing his true colors."

His true colors in a Joseph costume, Ruby thought.

"He just abandoned me at Goose Lake," Ruby then recounted. "I didn't accept his proposal so he swam off and left me alone. I've known him for a week and he's already proposed!"

"He must really like you because I never got any marriage talk from him," Jenny laughed. "He was hinting at it but never followed through. And that's just fine because I'm a quiet girl at heart. I only enjoy reading about adventurous types in books or seeing them in movies—which is how I first ran into my husband, at the movies. He's the projectionist at the theater in Royal Bend and one night he had a special marquee made up for me with WILL YOU BE MINE on it."

"Now that's a love story," Ruby complained. "Not the bumpy wagon ride I've been on."

"Couldn't you ever think of marrying Ben?" Jenny suggested hesitantly. "He seems like such special raw material, like how Michelangelo said he knew his statue of David was there inside waiting for him inside that big slab of marble."

"What in tarnation!" Jasper interrupted, sidling over and immediately wiping away two drops of water and a fleck of chopped peanut from the otherwise spotless soda fountain counter. "We leave you girls alone for a few minutes and you're already discussing naked statuary?"

"We were, but in our minds we always imagined David with a fig leaf," Ruby said.

"Or more like with a brown suede hat and those baggy pants Ben wears tied around his waist with a rope instead of a belt," Jenny added, and then she and Ruby laughed and Jasper shook his head and went to go play peek-a-boo with Alma and Charlotte.

Ruby waited along with Jenny at the train station so that Jenny and Charlotte could catch the evening run and head back to Royal Bend. It was nearly seven-thirty but the sun was still strong and Jenny turned the baby carriage away from the glare of it.

"You most likely won't have to see Ben much longer," Jenny said. "He's bound to take off someplace soon, especially since things aren't panning out with you. After he and I parted ways he went to Colorado and got a job in a silver mine. He came back the following June, but by then I was married. Uh-oh, speaking of the devilish beekeeper—here he is now," she murmured, pointing further down the platform.

Ben strode over to them defensively. "What are you hens clucking about?" he demanded.

"How we hate men who call women hens," Ruby said. "And who leave women stranded at lakes miles from home."

"Ben, how are you?" Jenny graciously interceded. "This is my daughter Charlotte—she's sleeping but you can take a peek if you'd like."

Ben hunched toward the baby carriage and peered in at Charlotte.

"Sure is an angel," he praised. "Especially since she hasn't learned to talk back yet."

The train rolled in and Jenny gently picked up Charlotte while Ben and the conductor lifted the carriage on board.

"Ruby, it was so nice to meet you and let's try to visit again soon," Jenny said, somehow managing to talk and walk and keep her daughter asleep despite the clang and rattle of a waiting train. "Ben, it was a pleasure to see you too and I hope you're reading lots. Bye-bye!"

She waved and they waved and the train moved on.

"That Jenny's a peach," Ben reflected. "I should've snatched her up when I had the chance."

"Oh well, your loss is her gain," Ruby said, turning to leave.

"That's right, keep sassing me," he retorted. "That'll smooth things over. I swear to blazes, why can't you be more like your Aunt May?"

Ruby then replied that if Ben hadn't already read H. G. Wells' *The Time Machine*, he should borrow it from the library then find out how to build a similar contraption so that he could go back fifty years and marry Aunt May himself.

"Don't think I wouldn't!" he yelled. Ruby kept walking. "You want a ride?" he offered but she didn't turn around. Any decent man would have followed her, she felt, and persisted and apologized for the afternoon's upheavals and making her walk so far before, but Ben did not follow and therefore she decided that it really was time for her and Mr. Greenlee to be through.

Though she wasn't a regular churchgoer, Ruby had promised Aunt May that she would come to the Sunday School pageant and see Joseph in his colored finery along with the rest of the short skits. On Sunday morning, however, she still felt caught up in a funk of confusion over Ben and thought it might be best to avoid any contact whatsoever. She stayed home and swept the house with a new broom instead, the stiff, springy bristles whisking out a surprising amount of dust and cobweb fuzz. She played *Shaking the Blues Away* on the phonograph while she cleaned, and she was so caught up in shaking and brooming her troubles into a dustpan that she didn't hear Ben at the screen door.

"Oh, what now," she muttered, though she let him in and asked how the pageant had gone.

"Real good," he said. He was wearing the same clothes as when she'd first met him and she also noticed that he was carrying a rucksack type of bag. "The costume got plenty of compliments, and your Aunt May was sure to let everyone know you were the one who'd sewn it up."

"Are you going on a trip?" she asked, feeling an odd combined twinge of sadness and release. Jenny had predicted that he'd be heading for someplace soon and she was right; Ben said that he was off to Mexico, with an indefinite return.

"After I leave here I'll hop one of those westbound boxcars and see if I can't make it to Chicago, then I'll start working my way south then across Texas. Then Mexico it is. Or if not Mexico, pretty damn close to it on the California border. That's where I like being best, on the border of both places. I haven't felt much at home here since I came back from Colorado back in '27. My brother's too itchy about having the stills and the hives all to himself, so I might as well just head down there. Better weather, freer living."

He picked up the stub of one of the beeswax candles he had given her and examined what was left of it moodily.

"Doesn't seem like anyone'll miss me either," he said, but it wasn't completely a ploy for attention and seemed more of a flat statement.

"Ben, plenty of people in Bright Bend care about you. And Aunt May will miss you terribly," Ruby argued.

He grinned. "That might be true and I'll miss her. Take a peek at what she gave me for my trip. Isn't she the best?"

He opened his bag and pulled an old biscuit tin now filled with layers of what Aunt May called traveling treats, or dates stuffed with pecans or candied fruit and then dusted with powdered sugar. My goodness, she sure is fond of this screwball, Ruby thought.

Ben offered a date to Ruby, ate one himself, then he put the tin back in his rucksack. "She'll miss me, but I suspect her great-niece can't wait until I've vamoosed. Especially since you won't let loose of that broom, like you're about to shoo me out the door."

"Nothing of the sort," Ruby said. "Would you like some iced tea before you leave? I'm out of coffee so we can't have that."

"You really think I'm going?" he prompted.

"Aren't you? Off in search of your Mexicali Rose?"

He looked at her intently, then nodded. "Yeah, I need to do a little wandering. Let's go out on the back porch and talk about it—I want to see how my handiwork's holding up."

They dragged two kitchen chairs onto the porch and sat surveying Ruby's flat patch of yard and the shimmery-leaved poplar trees that separated her place from old Henry Gwynn's.

"This is splendid," Ruby praised. "So sturdy, and such a deep shade of blue and so well-painted."

"I guess I did a pretty good job at that," Ben agreed, until he bolted out of his chair and examined some black pellets near the porch steps. "Aw, hell! A whole mess of squirrel droppings. I ought to pop that bushy-tailed rat with my shotgun before I leave here. He's been goading me on all week."

"I haven't seen that squirrel in days," Ruby said, and it was true—she wasn't just covering up for her ally. Ben returned to his iced tea reluctantly, scraping at the honey at the bottom of the glass.

"This is mine, right?" he asserted. "I saw you've got a jar of Jersey honey in your cupboard but Jersey honey's rarely as fine as what we make here in Pennsylvania."

"It is yours and yours is better," Ruby said. Ben took out a pipe and tobacco pouch, filled the pipe bowl and lit it with a wooden match. He scraped the match against the hardened bottom of his boot and it flared up right away, because Ben was just that type of person who could light matches with his shoe. Ruby closed her eyes and inhaled the spicy smell of his pipe while a breeze drifted across the yard and rustled through the poplars. This was pleasant, she had to admit. If they could somehow always be like this, he would be an unusually ideal mate.

"You don't smoke cigarettes, do you?" Ben asked.

"Maybe one every six months," Ruby said. "It's not a habit."

"It shouldn't be," he insisted. "A woman with a cigarette looks so cheap—I can't stand it."

"What about a man with a cigarette?" she inquired.

"Just a man smoking," he shrugged. "Nothing more or less."

And there was a reminder of how they never could seem to stay peacefully compatible. She tried not to laugh.

"It's big cities that corrupt women," he went on. "I don't even like visiting cities myself. Everybody's trying to prove this or be that and nobody's listening to each other. Along with heaps of trash and horse manure on the street and filthy air."

"Maybe," she had to concur. "But there are also lots of smart people and things to see—and there are books being written in cities and you like to read books, right? And there are restaurants full of food from different countries, just like you like to eat, and there are ideas and debates and theories, and you've got plenty of those yourself, Ben."

"I suppose," he conceded. "It sounds better when you describe it. You ought to take me round Philadelphia someday and show me the good parts. Of course, I might just get married in Mexico and that'll be it for us," he advised. "Being with you made me start wanting to have a wife and I like those girls down there a whole lot. You look close enough to some of them, like in that calendar I have, but those women are plenty different. They respect a man. You American girls just want to run us down and sass back to everything we do or say. And I may understand bees and their society but I still don't take to the notion of one queen bossing around all those drones. Poor dumb bastards."

Here Ruby excused herself to refill their iced tea glasses and to take a spoonful of honey like she had in the earlier part of this particular spell step. Not that she wanted to permanently keep from mouthing off, but she just wanted to finish this farewell without another argument. She could hold her tongue if she knew it was only for another half hour or so, and if she knew that she would not be hearing these opinions for the rest of her life. So she smiled and gave Ben more sweet tea, and she stayed sweet until he eventually rose to leave.

He idled on the front porch for further rumination and some vague promises that he might be back to see her sooner than she'd expect, and that they might find that distance makes the heart grow fonder.

"We might," she allowed, though the honey was wearing off again. "If you lose a few of your very fixed opinions."

"Or you lose a few more of yours," he challenged.

She knew that the goodbye kiss would be the true ring of fire and it was honestly the most searing kiss she'd ever experienced.

"Time," he said, coming up for air. "Could be we need time. Like remember that orange cordial we had after dinner the other night? It's too raw and harsh when you first start making it, then after time the sugar and orange peel and grain alcohol work together."

"That was delicious stuff," she whispered, still clinging to his shirt.

"Might happen for us," he reasoned.

Finally they pried themselves apart and Ruby asked Ben if he'd like her to walk with him to the freight rail tracks.

"No, I made you walk enough when I left you at Goose Lake," he said, extending an apology at last. She had never been so happy to see someone go away while in the same skipped heartbeat wishing that they'd reconsider. It was a ridiculous paradox, just like Ben himself.

She did walk him at least to where the end of her drive met the dirt road, giving one last tug on his sleeve while he offered a quick salute before loping on. Then she turned back toward the house, both laughing and crying of course, but laughter won out over tears when she looked up at the peak of her shingled roof. There was something up there looking almost like a weather vane; it turned out to be Ben's nemesis squirrel, now watching him go away. After a minute, the squirrel scrambled down and returned to its favorite tree, and from that point forward, Ruby couldn't help but notice that the thing never made any excessive noise or screeched again—and it also never left any more special black pellets on the porch.

Place a freshly baked pie of the choicest summer fruit upon your sill to draw the finest man to your home.

❧   ❧   ❧

For the faith and patience that sustain love, search the hills for hyssop and leave a bound bundle at your door to bring love knocking.

III.

❀

The July spell step had Ruby moving forward past Ben and making a pie of the "choicest summer fruit," which she was supposed to leave upon her windowsill to cool and lure in a delicious love. She was getting rather good at pie-making, though baking a pie in summer heat wasn't the most fun she'd had in her life; she did as instructed, however, and produced a ripely delectable strawberry pie with a perfect lattice crust and crimped edges. It was a pie worth taking a picture of, only she didn't have a camera. It was a pie that she placed on the windowsill and let the south wind carry the delicious scent of to whomever, and it was a pie that disappeared about half an hour later while Ruby was washing the rolling pin and scraping the hardened dribbles of strawberry juice off the bottom of the stove. She thought at first that it might have been squirrels or even someone's wandering dog or children at work, but a glance around the yard showed no knocked-over pie tin or traces of pie, just pure pie thievery.

"Son-of-a—" she began, disgusted, but then she paused and simply said dammit. And she'd be damned if she made another pie just to have it stolen, unless of course her true delicious love was a railroad tramp. She then changed her mind and contemplated making another pie, but this time filling it with nasty things like salt instead of sugar and a sawdust crust. Maybe some eggshells and a coat button or two. Soap slivers. Castor oil. It was a grand plan, and while she was dreaming it all up on the back porch the empty pie dish was snuck back onto the windowsill with fifty cents placed neatly inside.

When she reported the whole story to Alma later, Alma guessed that the pie had been snatched by Henry Gwynn, Ruby's crazy old man neighbor.

"He's not above taking a pie, but he'd be decent enough to pay for it and bring back the pan," Alma said. "And for you to get two quarters out of that skinflint is a big compliment. He must have really enjoyed it."

"Unbelievable," Ruby sighed, shaking her head. She thought of confronting Mr. Gwynn and asking if he'd filched the pie, but he'd just answer the door in his ratty union suit and be all twitchy and defensive and it was too nice a day to enter his sad, musty world. "But never mind, I don't care—unless this dumb spell says I have to marry him now."

"Well, he is available," Alma laughed. "And he wasn't always such a strange old scarecrow. He had a thing for my mother way back when, everybody knows that, and she wasn't too repulsed by him. If Dad hadn't finally come home from traipsing around Nova Scotia, I'll bet Mom would have married Henry Gwynn and he'd have a real home now and might take a bath at least once a month."

Ruby nodded, wondering about something. "Alma, I used your mother's pie recipe," she said. "And Henry's always been sweet on Aunt May, so he just happened to get caught up in the pie love magic. He probably smelled it and couldn't stop from coming over and taking it for himself. Like once upon a time, that pie should have been his. It was all crossed wires, like when a switchboard operator plugs you into the wrong line."

"That's such a generous attitude, Ruby," Alma praised.

"My attitude is generous," Ruby agreed. "But I'm not rolling out crust and slicing any more strawberries and waiting for a handsome escaped convict to show up—I can't go through that heartbreak again."

"You were hoping for a convict?" Alma asked. "Like maybe a bank robber or a murderer? Life isn't exciting enough for you here?"

"A convict who's been wrongfully imprisoned," Ruby elaborated.

"But only a handsome one," Alma reminded.

"Of course he has to be handsome," Ruby joked. "Why else would we fire up the oven and bake pies in July? Then I can help him clear his name—it'll be terribly romantic."

"He ought to have black hair and an iron jaw," Alma went on. "I knew a boy in high school who looked like that and he was just a dream."

"Is Iron Jaw in jail now?"

Alma pursed her lips, thinking. "I lost track of him when I met Jasper, but I seem to remember talk about his becoming an accountant. But if we're lucky he might have been accused of embezzling—come on, Ruby, make another convict pie and let's see if he comes crawling out of the woods in leg chains."

Ruby slumped on the sofa and propped her feet up on someone's old traveling trunk, which she had found in the shed and now used as a coffee table. "No, I hung up my apron, I'm done for today," she said. "I'll just wait until the next spell installment. Do you know what it happens to be or will you turn into a ladybug if you tell me?"

Alma smiled mysteriously. "I believe it has something to do with hyssop."

"Hyssop?" Ruby repeated. "What's that?"

Alma smiled again. "You'll find out soon enough. In a couple of weeks you'll know exactly what hyssop is—and exactly where to find it."

The full moon arrived and so did the quest for hyssop, which Aunt May showed Ruby an illustration of in her encyclopedia of herbs and flowers, as otherwise Ruby would have had no clue what to look for. It was a leggy plant with blue blooms, referenced to in the Bible and often made into a syrup to fight off chest colds. In the love spell, the search for hyssop symbolized faith, because it wasn't always easy to find. Aunt May was about to send Ruby hyssop-hunting in the mountains with a compass, a few slices of raisin bread and a canteen of cold cider, but just as Ruby was nervously beginning her journey, Alma hurried to walk alongside her and offered an alternate option.

"Listen, you could be wandering around for a week trying to find a patch of hyssop," Alma said, once they were out of earshot of Aunt May. "In Mom's day, most girls knew the woods very well because they lived in the country and walked everywhere. But you didn't grow up in Bright Bend and you haven't been traipsing around here all your life, and to be honest I'd have trouble finding hyssop myself."

"So how did you find it when you did the spell?" Ruby asked.

Alma shrugged. "I only had to go through the first step of the spell, with the pinecone and the dream. I dreamed about a man with a pocket watch, remember? Then I met Jasper two days later and we were engaged by the end of that week."

"How perfect," Ruby mocked. "And here I'll be doing this thing until the bitter end, I just know it."

"That's why I'm trying to help you out, dummy," Alma reminded. "See, Lewis Tyler's mother lives cattycorner from me and she has a real nice flower garden, and she grows hyssop alongside that garden because hyssop lures in butterflies and bees and helps everything get pollinated. I told her you needed hyssop for a special syrup and that you'd stop by for some later. She's going to a christening in Elmira anyhow so she won't even be there, but she said she'd leave her shears out for you to get your cuttings."

"Should I just head straight for Mrs. Tyler's?" Ruby suggested.

"You could," Alma said. "But you ought to at least make an effort to find the real deal. Take a walk for about an hour or so, enjoy the day, give it your best shot, then head back here and get your cuttings."

"You're right, I should at least make an effort," Ruby agreed, feeling perkier now that she knew there'd be a definite end to the search.

It wasn't a bad walk at all and Ruby didn't even lose her bearings, though she did end up way too far to the west and found some brush so thick she could barely get through it. By the time she headed back down the mountain her legs were full of cuts from the tangled branches and weeds and her face and bare shoulders were sunburned, but that was nothing that a long bath and a splash of witch hazel wouldn't cure. She had walked for three hours, not just one, and figured she had fulfilled her obligation—plus she was getting close to that time of the month and feeling crampy and not inclined to communing with nature if she didn't have to be.

"God bless Alma," Ruby said, once she had taken her hyssop slips from the patch by Mrs. Tyler's fragrant garden. Such lovely roses and daffodils, snapdragons, irises, and a bunch of other flowers Ruby didn't know the names of. She took a shortcut from Mrs. Tyler's yard back to the road that led to her own house, stopping by the creek to cool her feet. She had been walking constantly now for hours and when she finally did stop moving and stood alongside the smoothly rushing water, splashing her sunburned cheeks as well, she felt worn-out and about ready to faint. She sometimes got like that when she was riding the red tide and overexerting herself, just rundown and weak and wobbly, and she hoped that she wouldn't topple over. Otherwise this was as pretty a spot as Mrs. Tyler's garden, with the tall high trees all around the creek and their green shadowy leaves, the soil by the water rich and black and the water itself glinting in the late afternoon light.

Ruby balanced herself with effort and got ready to make that final half-mile trip home, though she was still woozy and even imagined that she saw some thin blond man sneak up and point a camera in her direction. She thought she'd glimpsed him out of the corner of her eye along with a huge dragonfly, like the dragonfly of her dreams, but when she went to investigate the dragonfly was really a stiff-legged grasshopper and the blond hallucination and his camera looked more like a fallen tree branch than anything—or anyone—else.

She had to bind the hyssop with string and place it by her front door, where it filled the air with a minty sharp scent until it began to wither and dry up. She told Aunt May that she had just happened upon Mrs. Tyler's patch of garden hyssop after an unsuccessful search—without mentioning any of Alma's guidance. Aunt May had seemed suspicious but had otherwise let the matter drop, adding with a far-off smile that in her case, it was the hyssop that had brought Uncle Zerah home to her.

"That was my last step to the spell," she recalled mistily. "And maybe it'll be your last step too."

Ruby doubted that such a romantic miracle would occur, but she kept quiet. She did, however, ask Aunt May whether anything had happened with the previous step and Aunt May's own making of the pie.

"You said you baked a strawberry pie then, like the one I made," Ruby persisted. "Did anything happen with yours? Did Henry Gwynn eat the pie maybe?"

"No, your Grandma Ruby found Luke Pritchard with her pie, but mine just stayed on the sill for a few hours. Then Daddy came back from fishing and said he was starved and wanted pie right away. My mother told me to let him have it, because enough time had passed and that obviously wasn't the right part of the spell for me. And Henry Gwynn, why would you bring him up?" Aunt May asked, looking curiously pert for a moment. "I already told you we only courted for a short while and he was too uppity for my tastes. He kept saying he wanted to marry a city girl and build a big house and become rich and that I was too *country* for him. Imagine that! Somebody who ended up living in a shack eating nothing but oatmeal and beef jerky once had the gall to call me countrified. Of course he did lose money in a bad investment," she reflected. "And his wife died in childbirth along with the baby, and he wasn't ever the same again. I suppose he has his reasons for shutting out the world."

Ruby sighed and looked through the window over at Mr. Gwynn's weirdly tilted home across the meadow and almost wished she hadn't asked Aunt May for details, because now she'd have to feel exceptionally sorry for him. She made another pie the following morning, so that he could have something to eat besides oatmeal and jerky and so there could be a little joy in his life, but when she set the dish to cool on the windowsill another man strolled up. She was totally surprised and almost screamed, hoping she wasn't really about to meet up with a convict; this person seemed friendly, though, and not in any sort of escaped prisoner hurry or panic. After getting a closer look, she wondered if he was the man who had taken her picture by the creek the day before.

"Yep, that was me," he admitted. "I didn't want to let you know I was there because you looked like one of those wood nymphs in fairy tales, and if I'd told you that you'd maybe think I was cracked in the head. But I am not cracked in the head," he added earnestly. "I'm an artist. I know sometimes those things go together but not in my case, or at least not yet."

Ruby was still inside the house listening to him through the open window, mystified. Because he seemed capable of appearing and disappearing into thin air, and because had truly crept out of nowhere just now. He was fair-haired with slightly sharp features, about her age in years, slim and rangy and reminding Ruby of a cowboy—not that he was wearing a cowboy hat or boots or carrying a lasso and saddle, it was just how he tended to lope along quietly. And how he tended to drawl over his words, though that seemed to be because he was originally from Kentucky.

"I've been walking north since April," he explained. "I guess I eventually want to get to New York but not until the fall. I'm not fond of cities in summertime. I like the country better then."

"You've been *walking* from Kentucky," Ruby repeated. "Isn't that hundreds of miles away?"

"Sure, but it's not so tough," he said. "You know because I said I'd been at it since the beginning of the spring, and I'd just walk a ways each day then stop, work odd jobs and camp out in a farmer's barn, do some sketching or take pictures, walk more, work more. By the way, my name's Eli Turnby, if you'd care to know that fact. And you're Ruby, I know that myself, because I helped paint this house with Ben Greenlee. We'd been hanging around for a month or so beforehand and worked pretty good as a team together. Or excuse me," he laughed. "We worked good as a team as long as I did most of the laboring while Ben sat under a tree, reading or sleeping."

"Did you have a squirrel bothering you?" Ruby wondered, but Eli said no, there hadn't been any squirrel of note.

"Ben was real lazy when it came to painting," he continued. "And he only started fixing the front porch after he heard you might be coming. Then once you did show up, he told me to hit the pike because he didn't want any competition. But I guess you told him to hit the pike yourself."

"Not exactly," Ruby said. "He hit his own pike."

"It's no matter to me," Eli continued. "After I took off from here I ended up doing some watercolors of the Nicholson Bridge and they were good enough for me to sell to a picture postcard company. And Ben's gone now anyhows so it's all turned out okay."

The Nicholson Bridge was a local wonder, a splendid arching engineering marvel that loomed above the landscape and even looked like a golden vision if you saw it in the right light. Treasure was rumored to be buried at its base. Ruby wondered if this Eli was telling the truth and had done the postcard watercolors. The part of the story about Ben being lazy and domineering seemed true enough, however.

"Would you like your house painted?" he then asked. "That's why I was stopping by, to see if you were interested."

"I thought you said you'd already painted it," Ruby answered, confused. "Does it need another coat?"

He smiled in a way as sharp as the lines of his face. "No, I mean painted like would you like a picture of your house done? Some folks take to having a portrait of their house to hang inside the house. Rich people especially are always hanging up paintings of their regular houses and their summer houses, and of course pictures of themselves. And let me tell you, if you do a painting of a rich person, you'd better make them look better than how they look in real life if you want to get paid."

Ruby could see now how Eli had some striking dark blue eyes. Not the true blue of Aunt May or Alma's eyes, or her father's smoky bluish-grays, but more of a deeper secretive color, like the indigo of dusk or shadows.

"I don't think I need a picture painted of the house," she said, yet then she thought about a photo taken of her father from when he had just graduated law school and what a special portrait that would make. Her mother had had her portrait painted when Ruby was about eleven, and she had also seduced the portrait painter. After Isabel's death, the painting was kept in her father's room behind the door covered with a sheet, though after his death Ruby had torn through the framed backing, cut the portrait into strips and dropped everything into the trash bin where it belonged.

A portrait of her father now would even the score and preserve the right image for all eternity. Ruby also wanted to test Eli's supposed artistic genius out and see what he came up with. She mentioned the idea to him.

"Let's get to it," he agreed. "I won't charge you either, because I took that photo at the creek yesterday and I can turn that into a fine painting. Even with all the modern art happening today and nothing looking like it really does anymore in pictures, there's plenty of folks who still want scenes with wood nymphs or girls who seem like they're part of a daydream. Though I won't paint you in that same checkered dress you had on, I'll put you in more of a gauzy outfit. You'll be partly nude but not totally. You don't have to pose naked either—I can figure things out enough on my own."

"Gee, thanks," Ruby said, not sure whether to laugh or slam the window shut and call the Sheriff.

"I'll work on your father's portrait first if you'll give me a week's worth of meals and let me stay in your shed back there," Eli continued, ready to close the deal. "I can turn that into a little studio. I've got my paints and brushes and a couple of canvases in the Ford, along with a cot to sleep on."

"What Ford? I thought you said you walked here from Kentucky," Ruby noted suspiciously.

"I did walk, that's no lie," Eli returned right off. "Except that after I made that postcard money, I bought a Ford from a fellow in Nicholson who wanted a newer one for himself. When I left Paducah, I had a change of clothes, a sketchbook and some pastels. Now I've got a camera, oil paints, brushes, canvases and an easel I made out of scrap wood. That's a lot to haul around. I'm figuring your next question will be where is that Ford now and where have I been staying since, and my answer will be it's over by the creek I took your picture at and I've been sleeping in Lewis Tyler's general store. Ask him to vouch for me, I don't mind. He had me do a painting of his mother's garden for her birthday and paid me ten dollars for it along with anything I wanted from inside the store itself. That worked out well, especially since I stocked up on coffee and ate steak every night while I was working on the painting, and I also got myself a crate of oranges for the road."

"Mrs. Tyler's garden is nice," Ruby said, smiling at the loop of coincidence. "With that patch of whatever growing next to it that she has—did you put that in the painting too?"

"You mean the hyssop?" he asked. "No, that's not in the picture because I went closer toward the roses. Are you partial to hyssop? I saw how you were carrying some the other day when I took your photograph."

"Hyssop? Oh, I like picking a bunch every now and then," she said vaguely. He had an artist's eye for detail, she had to admit that.

"Could I take a look at the photograph you'd like me to turn into a painting?" he prompted. "And I'm hoping you'll offer me a slice of pie, but I don't want to be pushy. But then again I've noticed that if you don't ask for what you want or speak up for yourself, you don't get much." He tilted his head to the side and looked closely at Ruby. "Your face is just about a perfect oval, you know that?" he praised. "I could paint a bunch of pictures of you."

"Uh, gee, thanks," Ruby said again, like she had when Eli had told her she didn't have to pose naked because he'd figure things out on his own. Like she still wasn't sure whether to grab her pie and run, or just to see where this hyssop-related adventure took her. She ended up letting Eli have two hefty wedges of the second strawberry pie after he had gotten his Ford with his sketchbooks and canvases and art supplies. And if the work he was showing her was his own, he was undeniably talented. She glanced through pages and pages of drawings of flowers, landscapes, deer, churches, men, women (mostly young, pretty and wood-nymphy women, Ruby noted), trains, clouds, houses, and the Nicholson Bridge. Those bridge sketches were especially notable and she wasn't surprised he had made a sale with them.

"I never went to art school," he said. "Just learned to draw from photographs and books and things around me. Though I did sit in on some classes on nude drawing at the art academy in Cincinnati. I couldn't afford to pay at the time, but the teacher was nice enough to let me pull up a chair and join the other students. The students weren't too hepped to have me there, but the teacher was a sport about it. I guess they figured they were paying for class so why give me a free ride. But like I said, you have to get what you can when you can get it."

"I'll bet the other students were just jealous over some ringer coming in and showing them up," Ruby said. She was looking over the nudes he was speaking of: nude man standing, nude man sitting, nude man hunched over with probably a stitch in his side from posing nude for so long. Then there was another thinner, lighter-haired nude man with a taut physique—Ruby took a particularly long glance at this nature boy, until she realized from the sharpness of the chin and the spare build that it was a nude self-portrait Eli had done. She closed the sketchbook with embarrassed reluctance then looked up to find Eli now sketching her, quickly and automatically.

"There you go," he grinned when he was done, raising the page so that she could see herself as she had been while looking over his other drawings. "How's that?"

"You and all your sketches are kind of remarkable, Eli," she decided ruefully. "And you ought to stop doing paintings for just ten bucks and free groceries or meals. You ought to charge much higher prices—right after you paint my father's portrait, of course," she laughed. "He'll be your last bargain deal."

Eli then showed her how he liked to practice signing his initials—EBT— which stood for Eli Baird Turnby. He had another part of the sketchbook full of that effort as well.

"It's important to have a signature that stands out," he said. "For the corner of sketches and paintings. That way folks will know in the future that they've got the genuine article. I like curving my B up high here. Gives it a sense of balance."

"That is a magnificent B," Ruby agreed.

Eli poured more lemonade from the pitcher Ruby had left on the table, refilling her glass as well.

"I may not be anywhere big today but I'll be famous soon enough," he advised her further. "I'm going places."

He was more factual than arrogant, his eyes so deep and dark a blue that she almost couldn't stop staring into them. However, when Eli mentioned how one of the first places he'd be going now would be back outside for a chew of tobacco, Ruby managed to shake off the charm of the indigo orbs and ask him to be sure to spit clear of the porch steps and not leave any dribble marks.

Despite Eli's talent, Aunt May did not approve of him hanging around and taking up Ruby's time of day. It was becoming clear that Aunt May was going to oppose any love spell suitor other than Ben, however, so that needed to be factored into her condemnation; she also kept harping on Eli's coming from Kentucky, a state which had never fully belonged to either the Confederacy or the Union. Aunt May felt that Eli's being a Kentuckian meant that he was possibly willing to take whatever side he needed to, and she further denounced his waiting until Ben had left town then slinking back in to chase after Ruby.

"My family—and that means your grandmother too, Ruby—was originally from Virginia, and we left there to come north because we believed in Mr. Lincoln," she recounted with pride. "We didn't sit on any fences."

When questioned, Eli said that both of his grandfathers had fought for the Union, but Aunt May wasn't convinced and muttered that Eli would claim his kin had fought for the South if someone from Savannah asked him the same thing. Alma, on the other hand, thought Eli had a gift and paid him his ten dollar rate—along with a new shaving brush, razor, shaving soap and several tins of hair pomade from the pharmacy—to paint a watercolor of Bright Bend's Main Street. Eli whipped out the town scene in about two hours, but Ruby could see how he worked more carefully with the oil paints he was using to do the portrait of her father. It was strangely thrilling to witness her father coming back to life on the canvas propped up on Eli's easel, and for him to be fleshed out in color as well, with Ruby helping to consult over the exact shade of Andrew J.'s eyes.

"Were they blue like mine?" Eli asked, squeezing small amounts from various tubes of paint onto his palette and mixing a few shades together. "Now mind you, what you see here will dry different on canvas. That's always the rule."

"No, your eyes are darker," she said. "Dad's were somewhere between cigarette smoke and the morning sky."

Eli laughed. "Alright then, let's see if I can manage that." He continued mixing then filled in the first coat, leaving the pupils blank because pupils were black and therefore needed to be done last. Still, without pupils her father looked blindly possessed, so Ruby excused herself to make lunch. She was creating a ham salad recipe that included chopped apples, sweet onions and mayonnaise, and she tossed in a pinch of nutmeg from her spice stash just for kicks. She had bought a bunch of apples from Lewis Tyler's store earlier and put them in a bowl on the kitchen table, and within minutes of being placed in said bowl Eli had done a warm-up-for-the-day pastel drawing of those same apples, and how the sun's light warmed their colors and cast a shadow along the tablecloth.

She sandwiched a heap of the ham salad in between some big sliced buttermilk biscuits and thought the result was quite tasty, and Eli evidently concurred since he ate three ham salad biscuits washed down with a quart of ice water.

"Ruby, you're just a pleasure to be around," he announced. "This is one of the best times painting a portrait I've had. I could lie and pretend I'm not finished but I'll be done soon, and I'll miss working in my shed studio out there—and I'll especially miss working here on your front porch. I like that the most, being out here painting while you're fixing lunch or supper or going about your business inside the house."

"I'll miss you too, Eli," she said. He was looking pretty fetching lately, his hair all sheened with the pomade he'd earned from Alma's Bright Bend watercolor and his face smoothly shaved with the pewter-handled razor Alma had given him as well. He took out a tobacco pouch and papers and rolled a cigarette, being careful to flick the ashes off the porch as she'd requested, and while he smoked it he regarded Ruby with as much interest as she was presently regarding him. His stare was too serious and too strongly blue, however, so she just smiled and went to wash the lunch dishes. A few minutes later he followed, standing beside her at the sink to dry the plates and glasses and silverware after she'd rinsed them.

"You think much about our old pal Ben?" he asked.

"I wish him the best," Ruby said truthfully. "I hope he finds what he's looking for. And I'll tell you one thing, he'd never be standing here with a towel in his hands helping me out now," she laughed. "He wouldn't be caught dead doing what he'd call women's work. I don't miss that about him."

"I don't mind wiping a dish every now and then," Eli smiled back. "I think it's best if we all help each other out whenever we can. Especially men and women, or more like man and wife—they ought to be like mules in a harness going along." He laughed, then shook his head. "I guess that's not the fanciest way to say it, but what I mean is it's best if two people pull together instead of against each other when they're married."

Ruby reached for the soap flakes nervously, wondering if he was about to propose or kiss her or tear off her apron—he seemed so tightly wound and ready to do *something* at any minute—but he just shrugged and dried his hands, picked up an apple from the yellow bowl on the table and went back to his painting on the porch.

The following day Eli said he needed to visit an "acquaintance" over in Albany and buy some art supplies while he was there. He had spiffed up to make the trip, wearing a gray silk-backed vest and a new shirt and trousers, though to Ruby he looked better and more at ease in one of his faded workshirts and paint-splattered overalls. He had finished her father's portrait and left it propped up on the table by the couch, and he said that when he came back he would take care of any last details and add a coat of varnish. He had done a marvelous job and by now Ruby was used to having the painting around and smiling through tears whenever she saw her father's youthful face. A face that had been decidedly intelligent, handsome in a pale way, the eyes staring ahead with the alert confidence of a twenty-five year old who'd had great hopes and dreams. By the time he had passed away he was even paler but still gauntly handsome, more cynical than spirited and only showing hope when he looked at Ruby.

"Mother was a raging idiot to treat you the way she did," Ruby sighed, addressing the painting directly. "You deserved so much better, Andrew J."

She found herself pining for Eli and wandered into his makeshift shed studio just to be among his things. While she was there she noted with a jolt that he had begun the painting taken from her moment by the creek, but he wasn't exactly sticking to his original idea of having her in a "gauzy outfit" and instead was painting her buck-naked. And slightly less in the bosom and rounder in the caboose than she truly was, though perhaps that went with his artistic vision. She stared at the work-in-progress, not sure what to think; she figured she didn't have the right to object because it was his creative expression, but she did turn Nude Wood Nymph Ruby toward the shed's back wall where only visiting mice and some nearby spiders could see it, just for modesty's sake.

Eli returned early the following evening and immediately knew the painting had been moved out of place. He came in to say hello while she was hanging some red toile curtains she'd made for the guest bedroom, startling her as usual with his quiet prowling walk.

"Were you ticked by that picture?" he asked, smiling.

She straightened the curtain rod, then stepped down off the chair she'd been standing on.

"Well, I was naked," she said. "That was an eye opener. You said you weren't going to have the girl be naked."

"I'm not," he explained. "But if you want to have any sheerness when you're painting, you do the figure first. Then you layer other colors over the flesh of the body, like you'd put real clothes on someone. I can show you how it works just so you don't think I'm lying like a rug. By the way, I brought you a present." He handed her a package wrapped in gold paper, which smelled as good as it looked.

"Eli, you didn't have to do that," she said, though she was thrilled to see he'd gotten her a box of French jasmine soaps. Alma had French soap at the pharmacy but only lily of the valley and rose, and jasmine was one of Ruby's favorites. "You're such a sweetheart!" she exclaimed.

"And you're so pretty," he said. "I could paint a hundred pictures of you. Would you ever consider posing naked? It sure would help me a lot."

"It'll take more than soap to get me to do that," she answered breezily, moving to the front room because she did not exactly want to be in a bedroom discussing nudity with him. He of course followed.

"I hope you're not offended," he kept on. "It just seems like you've got a modern way of thinking."

"I do," she agreed. "Which is why I've always thought it funny that we have all these naked women around in paintings. Society has a fit if a woman shows too much of herself at the beach or wears too short a dress, but it's okay if there's a naked gal hanging on a museum wall. Bowl of fruit, sailboats, vase of flowers, naked lady on a couch. Or naked lady in a harem. Or maybe a naked Venus standing on a big shell. And there are so many more naked ladies in art than naked men."

"We sketch plenty of naked men while we're learning," Eli said. "But when it's time to do a real painting, it's just a fact that naked gals are much nicer to look at."

"Sure, and those gals are especially nicer for you boys to paint," Ruby laughed. "You've got quite a special club going there. Paint or draw naked women for a living!"

Eli grinned crookedly. "So would that be a yes or a no to the posing question?"

"A definite no, simply on the grounds of decency, sir," Ruby sighed, pretending to be demure. "It's scandalous that you would even raise the question." She pointed to the portrait of Andrew J. "Especially in front of my dear departed father. Daddy, please don't blame me—it's this terrible wild-minded artist here suggesting such awful ideas. And incidentally, Mr. Turnby," she added to Eli, patting at her trim hips. "Your version of me is too fleshy in the derriere. I'd like that corrected."

"Well now, I wouldn't know if that's rightly so because I'm only allowed to guess what might be going on in that area," he laughed. "I can't change it until I see what I'm correcting." He then turned to her father's portrait and dipped his head. "Forgive me, sir, I'm about to grab your daughter because she has been tempting me for weeks and I'm not strong enough to resist anymore."

Eli moved forward and slid his hands around her waist almost like they were about to dance, only they didn't budge. His fingers inched upward along her spine instead, then caressed the slope of her shoulders.

"I'll bet your back is as smooth and white as milk," he whispered. "How's about you let me paint you wearing a red velvet dress with no back to it? With your dark hair and your pale skin, and the red velvet and the bare back showing all the way down to your bottom. That'd sell for a heap of money."

She surprised herself by kissing him then rather than waiting for him to kiss her, because his eyes were so strange and dreamy, like one of those cool lakes up in the mountains that you just had to jump into on a hot day. He kissed her wildly in return and seemed bound and determined to get a look at her bare back and other areas, until she stopped him and he nodded and took a deep breath.

"Listen, sugar," he said, getting hold of himself again. "I'm at a real crossroads now—I need to talk to you about something."

Whatever it was had Eli looking very perturbed, but it would also have to wait as Jasper had just pulled up in the driveway. He walked toward the house holding a catch of fish in one hand and a basket of corn in the other.

"Ruby, I've been evicted from my own home," Jasper complained. "Alma has her Town Sisters meeting at the house tonight and she shooed me over here and said you should fry up this catfish for supper. And steam the corn. And maybe concoct a dessert. Eli, of course I'd love for you to join us."

"I'm not cleaning and gutting those slithery things—that'll be up to you two," Ruby said. "But I'll be happy to cook them and make some rice and Creole sauce too."

Ruby breaded and fried the catfish and made a side of Creole rice, which was just white rice, chopped tomatoes, onions and peppers and a dash of Tabasco. She also did concoct a dessert of simmered pears with a brown sugar caramel glaze, and everyone appeared fairly stuffed when dinner was through. Eli appeared a shade moody too, however, and excused himself to turn in early on his cot in the shed. Ruby and Jasper played a few rounds of Twenty Questions after he'd left, then shortly before midnight Jasper said he ought to be on his way.

"Now make sure you tell everyone how we all had supper together and Eli behaved like a Boy Scout," Ruby teased. "And that there's nothing naughty going on around here."

Jasper's visit had clearly been a checking-in on the somewhat dubious situation of a young unmarried artistic man hanging around the shed of a young unmarried city-bred woman. Not that the young woman wasn't one of Bright Bend's own and related to the best citizens in town, but she did have some free-wheeling tendencies and had already been observed consorting with *two* different gentlemen in as many months. That's what Ruby guessed had brought about Jasper's impromptu dinner, and while Jasper pretended otherwise at first, he finally agreed.

"Just trying to keep control of the reins," he said. "Since it is something people will mumble about if it's not handled right. But we're handling it right." He winked knowingly while chewing on a toothpick.

"I'm not so sure that we are, Jasper," Ruby joked. "Because now there'll be talk about you and me and our illicit night of catfish and Tabasco. Don't try to use Eli as a distraction, we all know what a philanderer you are."

"I am quite the rogue," Jasper said, not missing a beat. He adjusted his glasses precisely. "When I walk through town you can hear the women sigh. And belch happily in relief if they've gotten some sodium bicarbonate from me at the pharmacy. By the way, when is the Kentucky Rembrandt going to be moving on? Wasn't his original plan to go to New York?"

"I thought it was," Ruby said.

"Looks like he's gotten a mite distracted lately," Jasper noted. "By yourself. And I don't care if you take up with him in the least, because he's talented but doesn't act all full of himself like plenty of other arty types—but you do need to get that fellow out of your shed and into a different residence until you're properly man and wife. It's just how the rules are out here and the fact is that people talk."

"Shoot, I don't want to be talked about unless I'm having the fun of sinning," Ruby complained, and Jasper smiled briefly.

"Doesn't work that way, my dear," he said. "Half the fun for gossipers and disapprovers is the suspicion. And the whispering and the mouthfuls of possible scandals served with tea and snickerdoodles in their spotless kitchens. We're not a mean-spirited community but people still are people and they like to sniff out a story. And in the case of some of the buffoons I play poker with, what they're not sure of they'll invent and fill in lots of smutty details. So let's not make it any easier for them."

He honked his horn as he drove off, the car's headlights glowing along the wooded road.

Good thing Jasper hasn't seen Eli's nudie creek-side picture, Ruby thought. She then ignored the fact that another light was glowing in the distance—Eli had his oil lamp lit in the shed, even though he'd claimed to be so tired—and instead she headed to bed, walking with morally upright posture through the house just in case the Mayor or his wife, Lewis Tyler or his mother, Hazel the town postmistress, old Henry Gwynn, the train station agent or any passing farmhands, drunks, or black-masked raccoons happened to be keeping watch.

The scent of the jasmine soaps Eli had brought her wafted into her dreams the next day and coaxed her out of bed to take an early bath. It was a sparkling summer morning, so bright that the chrome of the faucets gleamed and the porcelain of the new tub seemed even whiter than usual. The soap lather was creamy and fragrant, the water temperature deliciously not too hot or cold, and Ruby felt healthy and happy to be alive. She enjoyed her bath so much that she ended up snoozing amid the suds for about a half an hour, waking because a draft coming down the hall was making the door creak. She hurried out then and got dressed; she would have liked to lounge around in her robe and sip coffee for a while longer, but Eli tended to amble over for breakfast by nine a.m. and it was already quarter-till.

She decided to make French toast, since her bread had gone stale and that made it perfect for such a continental venture. She was dipping slices into a mixture of egg, milk and vanilla then dropping them onto a hot buttered skillet when Eli drifted in, punctual as always. He nodded and poured himself some coffee, watching her quietly. When the French toast was done he ate it without speaking as well, then he wiped his mouth with his napkin and cleared his throat twice.

"Do you recall my saying I was at a crossroads yesterday?" he asked. Ruby confirmed that she did recall him saying that, yes. "Then here's the story," he continued. "I'm picking up speed as an artist and I want to be a successful one. Now through my travels, I met a lady in Albany and she's from a rich family and she wants to be my patron. She's going to give me a place to stay and money to live off of, and she's going to introduce me to other rich folks who'll hopefully buy my work. The problem is that even though she's married, I don't think she'd care much for my hanging around with you. We'd have to do things on the sly or she'll cut me off."

Ruby was about to answer that she wasn't much for doing things on the sly, but Eli kept talking.

"You see, she's got the cash and the interest in me and she's in those rich people circles," he said. "Once you get into those circles, you've got a strong chance of doing all right. On the other hand, I have to commit adultery with her because she wants all that from me too. No getting around it. In the long run it'll be worth the bother, though, I'm sure. And if it's not me she's committing adultery with, it'll just be some other painter. Rich women can be like that," he advised. "They have lovers, and their husbands know they have lovers but that's because they have lovers too."

"Indeed. Thank you for sharing your knowledge of high society, Eli," Ruby said, shaking her head incredulously. She almost mentioned how her mother had had her own share of lovers, but she didn't want to open that can of peas just now. "I appreciate your honesty and hope it all works out for you."

Eli held up his hand, smiling. "Just a minute, sugar—I'm not through yet. That's only one direction of the crossroads, and now I'll explain how you're the other. Because you're a lot more inspiring to me and I could bluff my way out of the deal with the lady in Albany and stay here. I could paint and sell a slew of paintings of you, like I keep saying, and we'd have a mighty decent life. Only you're going to have to pose naked whether you like it or not and just get on board with my being an artist as the most important thing to us both. I'll sacrifice for you if you make it worthwhile for me."

The thing about Eli, Ruby guessed, was that he was so focused on and earnest about his work that he didn't realize how brash he sounded otherwise. In a sense, his not pursuing being a protégé was a huge concession to make, but she also guessed that she might hear about that concession constantly if she became the path taken on the crossroads. Or that with that type of single-minded purpose, Eli might leave her further down the line if he got another better offer. He affirmed this speculation with his next speech.

"The problem is that the Albany lady's got the loot and can pull the right strings, but I like looking at you and being with you and there's plenty of natural beauty around this place." He poked his fork thoughtfully into a puddle of syrup on his plate. "I don't like looking at her so much and it's going to be a tough one to keep romancing that face and body. Still, no matter what the case, I'm better off now than I was with my wife."

"Your wife?" Ruby repeated slowly.

"Yes, my wife," he shrugged. "And three kids."

She reached over to the stove and picked up the still-warm frying pan. "Eli," she said evenly. "Please keep talking and explain why I should not slam this down onto your head."

"You shouldn't because she was my brother's wife originally and I got railroaded into marriage after he got killed in the War," he retorted. "Nobody listened to how I kept saying I wanted to be an artist, they just insisted that I marry her because she was pregnant and it was my brotherly duty. I had no choice! I was nineteen years old and my folks pushed me into marriage, then she pushed me into taking a job in a shoe factory and I never could do any painting and drawing because I was wrung out from work. Then I said I don't want any more kids but she kept getting pregnant. Then she wanted a house and a car and was always spending all my pay, and I just had it, I left last March. I send cash back every now and then but I'm out of that trap and I'm never getting caught in it again."

He had tears in his inky blue eyes, though he wiped them away roughly with his shirtsleeve.

"I was in the War too," he murmured. "And I saw artists in Paris and I was as good as most of them. I told myself then if I survive this I'm going to get my share. Then I did make it through alive and with all my arms and legs, but first thing I hear about when I get back is here's your next obligation and we don't give a cold damn about your plans."

She watched him moving his fork along his plate again and had a feeling he was gloomily practicing his EBT signature—in syrup. And she just didn't know what to think.

"So are you going to clobber me with that skillet?" he asked.

"No, Eli," she sighed. "You're too complicated. I can't hate you, but I doubt that I could ever trust you either. I can see why you'd leave your wife, yes, but you also said that she kept getting pregnant and it seems to me that it takes two people to make that happen. You were doing your brotherly duty that way too."

"Well, she was *there*," he huffed. "I figured I ought to get something out of the bargain."

Ruby laughed then; she simply couldn't help herself. Eli took this as a promising sign and tried to put his arms around her, but she edged back.

"You like me, don't you?" he whispered. "Just in how I look and how we felt together yesterday when we kissed. Isn't that right?"

"Yes," she admitted. "But that's not all there is to it."

"Then what's wrong?" he persisted. "Don't you want to be my muse? You already are, you know."

"Thanks for the honor, but what happens when you find a prettier muse or when I get older?" she said, and then she noticed the bunch of dried hyssop by the front door. Hyssop that was supposed to give her a sense of faith. "I have faith that you'll be a successful artist," she realized out loud. "But I wouldn't have faith in you as a husband. I'm sorry."

"Do you really have faith that I'll do all right as an artist?" he asked, staring at her like a child.

"Absolutely," she said, and she noticed how this seemed to make him so happy that he didn't care about her lack of trust in him otherwise. Art was obviously just the whole ball of wax where Eli was concerned—and always would be.

He left later that afternoon, this time packing up his Ford to head to Albany instead of riding the train. He went for one last passionate kiss in the shed and after about four minutes, she resisted. Because he was a fierce but fine kisser, and because to use Eli's own logic she ought to at least get something out of the bargain.

Before he took off, he beckoned for her to come back toward the car window. "I wanted to show you this before I left," he said, opening up his sketchbook. "That's you taking a bath this morning. I saw that you were sleeping in there and snuck in, pulled up a chair and got my sketch. You never even knew it." He held up a key and handed it to her. "By the way, this fits both the lock on your shed door and the lock to your house," he advised. "Thought you might want to know that."

The sketch was lovely and he had correctly depicted her breasts this time, but she still tried to grab the book, rip out that particular page and tear it into confetti. He shooed her away and began to ease the Ford toward the road.

"You're gonna end up on a museum wall because of me someday!" he called, once he was safely out of reach. "Bet you a sack of pennies!"

"Make sure I have clothes on, EBT! Otherwise I'll take that sack of pennies and slug you with it!" she yelled back, and then she watched the Eli Turnby caravan drive away. And just like she'd been in parting ways with Ben, she felt a mixture of wistfulness and relief—along with a sense of not being sure whether she'd just been artistically exalted or gawked at by a sneak. And even after Eli had gone and there were no sketchbooks, easels, paints or painters in sight, Ruby still made a point to close all the windows and check the other rooms and closets for the Kentucky Rembrandt whenever she took a bath.

A strong marriage requires sacrifice and lack of vanity. Cut a long lock of your hair and tie to a ribbon, then hang the lock from the tallest tree to show that you are not silly and vain and will be a devoted, sincere wife. At day's end, place the lock in your hope chest.

IV.

❀

Not too shortly after Eli and his crooked easel had headed off into a painted sunset, Ruby found herself pounced upon by Annabelle Whist, the librarian's daughter. Ruby had gotten chummy with Mrs. Whist in her weekly library visits and learned that Mrs. Whist had a daughter and son about Ruby's age. Mrs. Whist was a widow who had originally come from Scranton and been married to a doctor; she played the piano divinely and knew enough about books and culture to run the library, though she had no formal library training.

The Bright Bend Library, however, was really just a converted old house willed to the town in 1917 by Lydia Lee Bailey so that Bright Bend could have a halfway decent library—instead of the hodgepodge collection of books that were kept in the post office, lent out and sometimes returned. Lydia Lee Bailey had published five poems during her spinstery lifetime and was therefore the town's literary genius. Miss Bailey had been fond of Ruby's father and expected great things from him, though she had accused him of being too *jocular* (Miss Bailey's word) at times. Ruby's father had found Miss Bailey's poetry sappy and too full of rosebuds and treacle, but he had never been jocular enough to tell her that in person.

In what had once been the Bailey parlor, Mrs. Whist had set up a reference desk and checkout area, while the dining room had been cleared and filled with bookcases that held fictional offerings. History and scientific subjects were upstairs in the former bedrooms, and the attic was where a small museum of the town could be found, with old photos of Bright Bend pioneers and Civil War soldiers and Miss Bailey's father shaking hands with President Cleveland when Cleveland had been hustling through Pennsylvania campaigning for votes. There were also withered back issues of the town paper and a sawdust-stuffed cougar, eternally snarling and ready to pounce. It was hardly the Philadelphia Public Library, but if you wanted a cup of coffee or a glass of iced tea from the kitchen in the back, Mrs. Whist would get you one—and she often gave cookies to the children who drifted in, to encourage them to visit again.

She kept a parakeet named Caruso by her main desk and was usually caught up in a good romance novel or biography herself, her ashy gray blonde hair in an un-librarian-like bob and her reading glasses linked to her person by a stylish beaded chain. Mrs. Whist had a warm, calm presence and a rosy prettiness even though she was in her late fifties, and had Ruby's father still been alive, Ruby would have been pushing Mrs. Whist upon him relentlessly. Not that Mrs. Whist needed help, because according to local gossip she was the special lady friend of Lewis Tyler. With that special friend status involving Mrs. Whist's going to Chicago at the same time that Lewis Tyler was there for a grocer's convention last summer—this wasn't public knowledge, but Alma and Jasper had the inside story. Lewis' wife Maisy had run off years ago without any explanation, and while Maisy did always send Lewis birthday greetings and asked about his health, the cards never had a return address and no one expected him to leave the porch light on for her anymore.

Mrs. Whist had first mentioned her daughter Annabelle with a slight, compressed smile, noting that Annabelle was close to Ruby's age and presently a schoolteacher in Ohio. Before that, Annabelle had been a schoolteacher in Baltimore and before that in Portland, Maine. Annabelle was strong-willed and full of more ideas and opinions than her school districts could manage, which was why she tended to be dismissed or transferred often. She wanted her students to love beauty and art and quote Shakespeare, or to draw pictures of clouds and write poetry while sitting under a tree. Unfortunately, she didn't want to teach such boring concepts as grammar or math or any of the state capitals, so parents and principals often became angry. Annabelle visited her mother on holidays and in the summer and when she was between jobs, though she tended to roll her eyes at Bright Bend and sigh about her Mrs. Whist's having moved there.

It was never clear just why Mrs. Whist had found her way to Bright Bend and taken over the library. There had been a vacancy after the previous librarian and fellow Ben-sufferer Jenny Walsh got married and gave the world little Charlotte, but it was suspected that Lewis Tyler had had something to do with Mrs. Whist's filling that void. Lewis hadn't owned up to anything, but he might have met Mrs. Whist through some Scrantonians and ultimately coaxed her over to Bright Bend. Mrs. Whist always murmured excuses about wanting to breathe fresh air and get away from the factories and mines of Scranton, but whatever the reason for her migration to Bright Bend happened to be, she did seem genuinely happy tending to her book haven and giving a free piano concert once a month. And having Lewis Tyler over for Sunday dinner, an event which he walked to and from with a slow, march-like pride.

Forever disrupting her mother's peaceful ways, Annabelle was a bundle of energy, criticism, hopes and dreams, talking on about books and writers, plays and the opera and everything you couldn't do in Bright Bend. She was blonde, plump, and always striving to be noticed and heard. Which she definitely was whenever she clomped around with her heavy tread, or when she raised her voice to full stage level even when making general conversation. She was eager to meet Ruby and didn't seem to notice that the pleasure wasn't mutual, like she didn't seem to notice that most of their chats were really just Ruby listening to Annabelle.

Annabelle was also one of those souls who know many fascinating people in other cities and towns, yet never seem to be with any of them. Evidently every other man on earth was in pursuit of her, and if they weren't in pursuit then they were ignorant or uneducated and not worth having. She was full of restlessness as well, a trait that worked in Ruby's favor because the restlessness and faultfinding shortened Annabelle's visits home. Annabelle had been talking about giving up teaching and moving to Philadelphia right near Ruby so that they could *frolic* around together when Ruby went back to the city in the fall. Or when she wasn't beating that drum, she kept trying to persuade Ruby to move to Greenwich Village—since Philadelphia was such a backwater anyhow, and so many of the world's greatest minds lived in New York. Ruby had pretended to have a burning desire to move to Pittsburgh instead and asked whether Annabelle would consider that option, and Annabelle of course was horrified and said that Pittsburgh was a terrible, dumpy, sooty city and anyone who wanted to live there willingly must be insane.

"I happen to find steel mills very exciting," Ruby had said, while Annabelle had looked at her incredulously. "And Pittsburgh is so close to West Virginia too! Just to go drive into the hills for the weekend and see the locals—that would be swell."

"Jupiter's orbits, are you kidding?" Annabelle had gasped. "Ruby, I realize that you come from Appalachian roots and feel the need to consort with beekeepers, but I had hoped you'd limit yourself to this dopey town and not seek out even worse areas."

"No, this feeling just gets stronger everyday," Ruby had smiled. "It's something deep and special inside me."

"Like a pernicious tapeworm, maybe?" Annabelle huffed, and then she gave Ruby the high hat and wasn't so friendly when she returned from her most recent New York sojourn.

Mrs. Whist's son Ned, fully named Edwin Samuel Langhorne Clemens Whist—his mother being a Mark Twain devotee—was another character, but not as intolerable to Ruby. For one thing, he was cute in a skinny, smart-boy way, with a clever spark to his gray eyes and a pleasantly wry smile. And while he was as full of ideas and theories as his sister, and while he could be just as obnoxious in interjecting those theories, Ned seemed to act more upon his words and to have a more humanitarian agenda. He was passionate about Socialism and vegetarianism, and he had started his career as a radical journalist who went undercover to expose horrible things going on in slaughterhouses and meat-packing plants along with unfair labor practices in sweatshops. Then he had lived on a cooperative work farm in Vermont, then he had taught English to immigrants, and now he wanted to start Socialist Vegetarian Societies in all major American cities.

He and Annabelle fought like two cats in a sack and reportedly had done so since childhood. She called him strident and unrealistic, while Ned called her a pudgy snob who thought she was Queen Brilliantina of Book and Painting Land—to use his exact words. At the Whist Sunday dinner Ruby attended, actual plates were hurled the across the table, with such screaming that Caruso the parakeet started screeching along with them. Lewis Tyler was not there, having been verbally attacked by Ned in his own store for selling butchered animal meat and for underpaying farmers who brought in their fruits, vegetables and eggs for sale. In truth, Lew Tyler tended to be generous with his payments to local farmers, and most people in town—including Mrs. Whist—would have been unsure of what to eat if he'd stopped selling chicken, beef and pork, but he tolerated Ned's tirade because Ned might be a future stepson and no one in Bright Bend ever took any of his raving seriously.

Also at the Sunday dinner Ruby attended—a meatless feast of beet salad, carrot bisque soup and potato-mushroom pie topped with sour cream—Ruby had something of a fashion mishap going on. The day before she had had to put the next phase of the love spell into action, this step involving taking a sizable (scalp to ends) lock of one's hair, cutting it off and tying a long ribbon around it, then hanging the ribbon with the hair from the tallest tree in sight from noon until dusk. The purpose was to discourage vanity and promote sacrifice, a part of the union between two souls that Ruby's mother had obviously ignored—though her father had certainly sacrificed enough. You then had to retrieve the ribbon and lock of hair, fold it up in cloth and keep it in your hope chest. Ruby did not have an official hope chest but was using an old hatbox from Wanamaker's instead, and just to prove she was hopeful, she had slipped a jar of orange blossom bath salts into the box with the intention of using them on her honeymoon. Or at least at some bathing point after marriage.

Unfortunately, Ruby's lock of hair kept disappearing, and on two occasions the ribbon disappeared too. After the third incident she began to wonder whether Aunt May was hiding in the bushes stealing curls and ribbons and having a good laugh, and after she had taken the fourth lock from as unobtrusive a spot as she possibly could, she crouched down on the porch and waited to see what was going on, discovering that the guilty party was a sparrow who kept swooping down and stealing the hair for its nest. With a couple of lengths of ribbon now even trailing from the tree's higher branches, like satin streamers. Upon being asked to stop, the sparrow became outright belligerent, but once Ruby sat underneath the tree with a badminton racket to gently shoo the bird away, she was able to successfully waste several hours of her life and finish the spell's next step. In the process, however, she cut too deep on the right side of her hair and left a strange and ragged gap by her ear. While she was examining it and experimenting with scarves and barrettes, Mrs. Whist called and asked her to supper the next day.

"My son Ned's in town. He heard me mentioning you to Annabelle, and he asked if I'd have you over." Mrs. Whist then lowered her voice. "I also think they'll behave better if you're our guest. And if they don't, well, then at least you'll see one heck of a Punch and Judy show."

Ned and Annabelle kept things controlled for about seven minutes, then Annabelle got snippy about special vegetarian dishes being fixed for Ned when her mother usually made Annabelle eat wretched chicken and dumplings because Lewis Tyler liked them so much for his Sunday meal.

"Along with those terrible pickled onions Lewis loves," Annabelle kept on. "And always the kind of pie or cake that he wants, never something special that might please *me*."

"You should skip pie and cake altogether, Annabelle," Ned noted. "And cut out rolls and butter and second helpings." He pretended to whisper. "You're getting a bit chubsy-wubsy. Buttons about to burst and all. Your chair's creaking so much I think it's ready to collapse."

This was when a plate of beets soared toward him, then he and Annabelle began hollering about who was the biggest idiot, then past incidents were dragged up and physical contact started and Mrs. Whist ushered Ruby out of the dining room to the yard. They sat at a small table near the lilacs and sipped coffee and ate cherry tarts, and Mrs. Whist ignored the chaos and noted how she wished there'd be a nice rain for the garden; the yelling inside continued, stopped, resumed, then there was a stomping upstairs and slamming of a door. Ned strolled out and joined them at the table, offering a remorseful smile to his mother and Ruby.

"Edwin, why did you have to mention her weight?" Mrs. Whist sighed. "You know how that riles her."

Ned shrugged. "She was complaining about the meal, Mother—and it was such a nice meal and I appreciate it so much and was enjoying every bite—but she's got to start up because the world wasn't revolving around her fat blonde head. I come home maybe every six months while she's here practically every other weekend—even though she hates being here so much, that's all we ever hear coming out of her yap—but she's got to start crabbing because we had some delicious food that everyone loved. Am I right, Ruby?" he asked, turning toward her with attentive politeness. In fact, it was amazing to see such politeness from someone who had been ripping into his own sister just a few minutes before.

"I did think it was a wonderful dinner, Mrs. Whist," Ruby agreed. "With food like that you don't even miss meat."

"Be careful now or Ned will try to convert you," Mrs. Whist laughed.

Ned sprang forward and bent down on one knee, pretending to propose. "I'm not just going to convert her, I'm going to marry her too," he joked. "She listens to what I say without yawning, she's already willing to give up meat, and she's also adorable with that bandana scarf she's wearing. You look like a gypsy girl, Ruby."

Oh, cripe, Ruby thought—Ned Whist is about to get sucked into this love spell. Not that he wasn't attractive and he seemed to have plenty of peppercorns in him, but would she have to become vegetarian and live in a shack, stop wearing perfume and go to a lot of fired-up Socialist rallies?

"Mother, keep Ned away from her!" Annabelle ordered from her bedroom above. "Ruby, don't even speak to him, he's insufferable. And ridiculous-looking—you might as well kiss a coat hanger."

Ned got to his feet and turned toward Annabelle. "Hark, what ugliness through yonder window breaks?" he called. Annabelle again hurled something—this time an old milk bottle now full of water and lilacs clipped from the bushes in the yard—and managed to graze Ned's left temple. She applauded and laughed and slammed her window shut, while Ned went through major gestures of pain and suffering and yelled that he probably had a concussion.

"Her aim really is getting better," Mrs. Whist observed idly, and then she asked Ned if he could please walk Ruby home. "Lewis is coming over with his mother and I'm going to play some Chopin for them."

"Don't you think that Ruby and I would like to hear the music too?" Ned complained, still rubbing his head.

Mrs. Whist began gathering up the fallen lilacs and bottle off the lawn. "Ruby might, but you'll just be sitting around all agitated waiting for me to finish so that you can bother Lewis again for charging too many pennies per gallon for gasoline. At least Annabelle settles down when I play the piano." She bent over to whisper in Ruby's ear. "Dear, I'm sorry to inflict Ned on you and if you'd like to escape, just blink three times and we'll come up with something else for him to do."

Ruby did not blink. Beyond thinking that Ned would most likely be an interesting diversion for the rest of the afternoon, she also didn't want to disappoint Mrs. Whist. She was growing quite fond of the librarian and her placid ways, and how Mrs. Whist was like both a friend and a mother. Ruby of course had never had much of a maternal figure in her life, and even just this moment of closeness with Mrs. Whist leaning over and whispering and touching her shoulder made Ruby feel a strange pang of yearning for something she had never known she'd needed.

The walk home mostly involved Ned talking about his past adventures and present beliefs, with a basic outline of Socialism and the health and humanitarian reasons behind a vegetarian diet. Along with the names of famous vegetarians like George Bernard Shaw, and a rundown of suitable protein substitutes. The thing about Ned, though, was that while he was so serious and focused on changing the world and talked about little else, he still had those slightly mischievous gray eyes and a quick sense of humor, and he was lithe and supple as an eel. He did tend to go on in too much detail about how pigs and cows and sheep were killed, and how besides promoting outright brutality, slaughterhouses were filthy and full of rats. When Ruby promised to read Upton Sinclair's book on the matter called *The Jungle*, however, Ned did subside.

They reached her house and Ned kept right on talking and following her in, and since he hadn't had any dessert at his mother's, Ruby made blackberry shortcake. Ned used the eggbeater to whip some cream with his sinewy wrists and they sat enjoying the shortcake and some coffee—though Ned noted how coffee pickers in South America were terribly exploited, but for now he would just drink the effort of their labor and do what he could to improve North America first.

Soon Ned flipped things around to asking questions about Ruby, like her relationship with her father and mother, her past boyfriends, what she considered to be her best and worst qualities, things she enjoyed doing and her favorite colors and books—to the point where it seemed more like a psychiatric interview than a conversation. Then Ned threw a total curveball, just when her attention was starting to drift and focus on a big Luna moth thudding against the screen window by the sink. He leaned forward, pursed his lips briefly, touched her arm with his slender fingertips and asked how she really would feel about marriage.

"I was only kidding when I asked you in front of my mother before," he explained. "But now I know you better and I think it's an excellent idea."

What was it about this kitchen that had all these men proposing marriage, she wondered. It had to be her father ghosting from beyond, like his spirit was probably sitting in the chair across from Ned smoking a spectral cigarette and sending crazy impulses through Ned's mind. The way he'd done with Ben and Eli—and the way he sometimes seemed to make the light bulb in the kitchen flicker and dim, just to show off.

"Yes, we know each other so much better now," Ruby laughed. "These extra two hours have really filled in the gaps."

"Now, don't be sarcastic—though I do appreciate that quality in you, like a tart twist of lemon," Ned smiled back. "Just hear me out. You see, Ruby, I've had a decent share of experiences and looked around, and when we met I felt a spark. I don't think marriage should be based on blindly raging passion, but I like feeling sparks. How about you?"

"I'm fond of sparks," Ruby agreed cautiously.

"I realize you haven't come around to my way of thinking yet," he continued, pouring out the last of the coffee for himself and savoring it still with a bit of guilt. "But I think you will. I think we have chemistry or energy that works well together, and that you'll be open-minded enough for me. We will have to live in a special community, though, that's just starting up on a small town on the Hudson in New York. Some friends of mine have been planning it for years and we've bought houses and land there, and we're going to quietly start a neighborhood that follows Socialism and let the effect ripple outward. And there'll be no meat consumption or organized religion. Which is why you and I will have to get married at City Hall, since a church wedding would be hypocritical."

"Hypocritical, of course," Ruby repeated, getting up to deliberately rattle some forks and knives around in the dishpan, because Ned's voice was starting to mesmerize her and she was afraid if she kept listening that she'd wake up tomorrow in the special Hudson River community as Mrs. Edwin Samuel Langhorne Clemens Mark Twain or whatever his name was Whist.

Before leaving, Ned slipped his arms around Ruby's waist and advised that she get some sleep and think about his proposal. They stood close while he gave her a short yet persuasive kiss, his hands gently on her hips pulling her in, then as gently letting her go. Ruby tended to attract more forceful types and she had never been kissed with such subtle power before. She even found herself clinging to Ned and not wanting to be let go at first, which seemed to be part of Ned's plan—to get her on a hook and lure her slowly in.

She was up late tossing and turning, finally falling asleep on the couch. Ruby had found that she could pull a fast one on insomnia by moving from a bed to a couch, and by tricking herself into thinking that she wasn't trying to doze off anymore, she was just reading a book or magazine. While her usual ploy was successful, she was woken a few hours later by Ned rapping on the front door; he was back again and wanted her to join him on a hike.

"Let's head up to Oval Lake," he said.

"Isn't that about ten miles away?" Ruby yawned, trying to fully open her eyes and clear the fogginess from her head.

"Four and three-quarter miles to be exact," Ned noted. "But it's a gorgeous day, and we can talk and walk some more. And eat breakfast in the hills." He was carrying a knapsack and what looked like a portable tent, shouldering both with ease. "I've got eggs and a frying pan and a coffee pot, and I made cornbread this morning."

"You made cornbread," she repeated. "Or maybe your mother did?"

He shrugged. "I made it myself and why wouldn't I? Cooking is simply a combination of the right ingredients and appropriate method of preparation, not any special female witchcraft. Though you do brew the best coffee I've ever had, so I'm going to let you handle that task. Are you coming?"

"Are we staying overnight?" Ruby asked, pointing to the tent. "Or maybe starting a Socialist paradise ourselves, kind of like Adam and Eve?"

Ned laughed. "If you're willing, I'm able," he said. "But the tent's just in case it rains. Or in case we want to hold a tent revival." He raised his hands and imitated a yelling preacher: "Glory be! Sister, step forward and let me heal your sorry soul! You've got evil in your eyes and even more down in your pajama bottoms! Smite your demons and shed those pajama bottoms right now! Hallelujah!"

That outburst and the fact that Ned looked so appealingly skinny yet virile prompted Ruby to agree to the Oval Lake hike, just as soon as she could chastely shed her pajama bottoms in the other room and also put on some good walking shoes.

While the trek to the lake did seem endless, with a short stopover to chat with a few railroad hoboes that Ned had somehow made the acquaintance of, the arrival was worth the trip. The sky was purest blue with billowing clouds and the lake rippled smoothly—though to be technical, it was really more of an oblong shape than an oval. When Ruby was younger she had come here with Alma and Aunt May and found it idyllic, but now Oval Lake had many more cottages and tents and rowboats and cars parked in the mud, as escapees from New York or Philadelphia found their way to the country for a long weekend. Things were still fairly sleepy at this hour of the morning, however, and she and Ned found a secluded nook that was pleasant enough. Ned built a small fire and scrambled eggs while Ruby made the coffee, and they ate and drank out of spatterware camping plates and cups and finished off Ned's surprisingly moist cornbread.

"Not too shabby, huh?" he demanded, watching Ruby relish her second piece. "I'll let you in on a cornbread secret I learned from the sweetest old lady named Eulalie who lives in Mobile, Alabama—leave the milk out overnight before you make it."

"And I will do that from now on," Ruby said. "Thanks, Eulalie."

Their peaceful nook was soon invaded by other hikers tramping by, and then the almost menacing glide of a man in a rowboat just about fifteen feet away. He was suavely handsome, his hair shiny with tonic and his face marked with what looked like the shadow of a black eye. He said hello to them both but stared hard at Ruby; he was drinking Coca Cola from a bottle but in the breeze they could smell whiskey mixed in. He let the boat idle, still watching Ruby.

"Want a ride, doll?" he offered.

"I'm fine here," Ruby said.

"You sure?"

"Float on, Slicker," Ned said tersely, then the Rowboat Romeo shifted his gaze to him.

"I'm giving your girlfriend a better option," he laughed. "So's she can get a taste of what she's missing."

Ned nodded. "You mean a date with a greasy pinhead?"

They glared at each other with hostility and while the man in the rowboat was taller and heavier, Ned's glare was more penetrating. Ned had encountered far worse opponents in his life, like strike-busting police and Pinkerton detectives and general rabble-rousers. The rowboater seemed to sense this, and he eased his oars back into the water and moved on.

"Ah, always a confrontation," Ned laughed once the interloper was gone. "And mind you, I wasn't being territorial, I just thought his behavior was rude."

"No wonder he had a shiner under his eye," Ruby said. "He seems like the type who picks fights. You weren't fazed, though."

"I try not to be," Ned said, brushing an ant off of Ruby's knee. "I have strong beliefs, so I've learned to fight for them with words and actions. Which helps me to stand up to blowhards and apes who think they own the earth."

More ants scurried here and there, and it appeared that they above all really owned the earth. They were fast moving and increasing in numbers, so Ruby and Ned decided to leave.

"They're just doing what they're supposed to," Ned conceded. "Ants don't have weekends or holidays—they're right up there with the bees in terms of community and hard work. Speaking of bees, I understand that you're quite chummy with Ben Greenlee."

"You know Ben?" Ruby asked, surprised at first, but then the puzzle pieces didn't seem too odd of a fit. Ben was smart and rebellious and had done his share of traveling like Ned, and if they hadn't met in Bright Bend they would have met in a mining camp or while riding the rails or at an anarchist picnic somewhere else.

"Sure. We've had some interesting talks and arguments, and he even got me plastered on his home brew last summer when I was visiting Mom," Ned laughed. "I generally don't drink and feel that alcohol has destroyed many a life, but if knocking a few back is going to bring down social barriers and allow a more equal exchange of ideas, I'll lift a glass or jug. But you and Ben—I heard there was some courtship going on. And maybe it's still going on? Am I stepping on Ben's turf? Because I'm not so sure I could take him in a fight."

Ruby shook her head and helped Ned rinse the spatterware plates and cups in the lake, then dry them with one of the dishtowels she had brought along.

"There's no more courtship," she said. "Ben and I disagreed on issues and he said he needed to go Mexico to find a wife because American girls were too full of themselves and sassy. Like every single Mexican woman is longing to bear his kids and wait on him hand and foot. I highly doubt that."

"Ben's just adhering to older customs and beliefs," Ned replied. "In a Socialist society he wouldn't act like that because he'd have had a more well-rounded education. We want education and expansive thinking to be as prevalent in the country as the cities. I am glad he hasn't been enlightened yet, though, because otherwise you might still be with him. He's attractive, you know? In a backwoodsy Davy Crockett way. And he's an enterprising soul and intelligent and adventurous."

"And mulish and pushy," Ruby added. "But I know, that's only because he's not a Socialist."

Ned had everything back in the knapsack by now and shouldered it and the still rolled-up tent easily. "I'm sensing a hint of mockery towards Socialism there, Miss Ruby, but after a week of learning you'll be more receptive. You need a crash course," he advised. "Naturally, I'll do the teaching—then after all that you should be ready to make a swift decision to get married and go to New York with me."

"Thank heavens!" she exclaimed. "I'm always so happy when men tell me what to think!"

Ned deflected her comment with a smile. "I didn't say controlled thinking, just enlightened thinking. Progressive thinking as well," he went on. "Would you like to consummate this relationship today? Physical tension can be such a troublesome factor—we make all sorts of bad decisions because we're confused by sex."

"Ha," Ruby laughed. "That sounds like a Socialist way of getting up a woman's skirt."

Ned reached around her waist and held her lightly yet insistently like he had last night. He then kissed her in the same manner and since no one else was near to see, he even discreetly moved his right hand up to her breast, fingering the nipple until it tightened. He had the heavy knapsack on and Ruby could have toppled him with one push, but she again found that she didn't want to move away.

"Go on, give it a chance," he urged. "Being together will free our minds—and I've made a point of learning how to be a very giving lover."

"Then that definitely won't free my mind," Ruby said, forcibly taking a step back. "How can you think your mind will be free either? Don't you feel that having sex just leads to wanting more sex?"

"I'll admit you're damned if you do and you're damned if you don't," he grinned. "But it's a much better damnation if you do, in my opinion. And how exhilarating that you're even talking to me about this, instead of slapping my face or pretending that only men have needs. I know we'll be fabulous partners when we do finally set up our tent together."

"Ned, you're starting to make my head hurt," she sighed, taking the tent herself so as to end any further tent-pitching speculation and so he wouldn't have so much to carry.

For the next three days she saw and listened to a barrage of Ned, with names like Marx and Trotsky, Fourier and Robert Owen thrown at her. And lots of explanation about ideal improvements in schooling and housing and shared ownership, and how capitalism was a failure and ignored the plight of too many poor people. Socialism could reduce crime, Ned claimed, because there would be equality and no haves and have-nots, and fewer perversions due to the elimination of puritanical mindsets. Then the vegetarian crusade started again, detailing how beyond even the cruelty to animals, meat-eaters were more prone to cancers and clogged arteries.

Ned talked while Ruby was ironing, cooking, cleaning or even sewing— just speaking louder over the rattle of the machine—then while she was picking up mail at the post office or taking books out of the library, which resulted in him being shushed by his own mother. Her secretly favorite part was hearing his healthy notions about sex, and Ned seemed to guess that he might win her over through lust and tried many times to take that approach. She knew she had to fight him off even harder then, however, so she generally started asking questions or contradicting his earlier remarks to make him stop doing exquisite things with his too-skilled fingertips.

"My father always complained that Socialism doesn't allow enough individuality or personal freedom," she murmured once, pushing Ned away with her left hand while holding him close with the other.

"You're twenty-nine now, not Daddy's little girl," Ned reminded, easing toward her again. "You should form your own opinions."

She moved her mouth away from his. "But you've been telling me all your theories for days and expecting me to just accept them."

He smiled calmly. "Yes, but I'm right," he said. "And once you're guided to see that, you'll know why."

"That sounds arrogant," she persisted, also buttoning her blouse back up and dragging herself free from his slinky charms.

"Well, that sounds unenlightened, to call me arrogant," he countered. "And just completely off the subject, why is a chunk of your hair missing here?" he asked, pointing to the spot where she had cut too deep to get her love spell lock.

"I had a curling iron accident," she lied.

"But why would you need a curling iron?" he wondered. "Your hair already has enough natural curl to it."

"Oh, sometimes you can use curling irons to straighten hair too," she offered.

Ned looked at her solemnly. "Ruby, you can't allow foolish notions held up by the warped mirror of American advertising to make you want to change your appearance. Imagine tearing out your hair just because it wasn't straight enough. And you're always opening up that compact and powdering your nose and cheeks—it's not necessary, you're fine as it is. You shouldn't be a slave to cosmetics. I understand that you worked for a women's magazine and your brain is still all sticky from the experience, but trust me, that is not the right path."

"Ned, trust *me*, I have oily skin and the powder is necessary—and I am not overly concerned with whether my hair is straight, curly or even combed sometimes. And right now I think I need some fresh air because my sticky brain is feeling even stickier," she rambled on, hurrying out and jumping on her bicycle to escape. Ned followed on his bicycle, however, and kept within talking distance for miles, until she veered toward home and collapsed exhausted on the porch. Her leg muscles were throbbing from so much frantic cycling and her ankles were scraped raw from riding through brush, and she could still hear Ned's voice talking even after she fell asleep on the porch chaise, despite the fact that Ned had propped her feet up on a milk crate, tucked a pillow behind her, then finally called it a night.

Sometime near dawn, Ruby woke to discover that she was still on the porch chaise and her right calf had knotted up into a mean charley horse. She walked it off in a few agonized circles, then hobbled into the house to go back to sleep in her real bed. She was making her way through to turn off the kitchen light when she heard Ned out back.

"Ruby," he called quietly. "Ruby, let me in now."

"My God," she whispered to herself. "He's not a dragonfly, he's a gadfly!"

She opened the door and was about to tear into him for harassing her at this hour, but her attention was diverted by the fact that he had just set a live chicken onto the kitchen floor. The hen flapped her buff-colored wings, then began exploring and pecking across the linoleum.

"Excuse me for asking, but what have we here?" Ruby began.

"Let me explain," Ned urged, closing the kitchen curtains. He was also carrying a suitcase. "I'm in some trouble and I'll need to leave town sooner than expected. I've been talking to some of the workers over at Bryant's Farms and letting them know that Wilson Bryant is exploiting them. He pays them next to nothing for a fourteen-hour day, fires them if they get sick, and makes advances at their wives and daughters. And since he's hunting buddies with the Sheriff, they have no one to complain to. And I've seen how he's cruel to his cows and horses and chickens—it's horrible. So he got wind of my discussions with the men and made some threats, and he could bash my head in with a shovel for all I care, but the particular threats he made were toward my mother and her home. Or toward the library, like burning it down. I don't want anything to ever happen to her or anything she loves, so I'm going away. That's all he cares about anyhow, getting me out of town."

Ned looked so unusually distressed that Ruby forgot her previous annoyances and the chicken in the kitchen and held him close.

"Don't worry," she soothed. "Your mother's got Lewis Tyler in her pocket and Lew Tyler is the most powerful person in Bright Bend. Wilson Bryant knows that and he's just bluffing."

"But I don't even want to tell her," Ned insisted. "I don't want her to worry for one minute or resent me for being her son."

"She'd never do that," Ruby said. "But maybe you should disappear for a while and just let Annabelle be the reason that people want to throw rocks through your mother's window. With threatening notes attached, like get that uppity gal and her highfalutin ideas out of here."

Ned relaxed into laughter for a moment and pressed his lips against her forehead. "You've made me smile at a very tense time, Ruby, and it's because of your strength of character that I'm giving you an extension. If you're not ready to commit to coming with me just yet, I will leave the offer open through the summer."

"Well, thanks, Ned," Ruby said, half-wishing he'd just cut her off so that she wouldn't have to keep torturing herself with the option. "And is the chicken leaving with you or does she also have the whole summer to decide?"

"That chicken is a symbol of freedom," Ned declared. "When I was leaving Bryant's main farm area, I felt terrible because I hadn't made the changes I'd hoped for and because all those animals were still going to suffer. But then this chicken came out of nowhere, escaped from her filthy prison coop, and she walked right up to me and I grabbed her and ran. She wanted to live. And I'm bringing her to you so that she can live and give you eggs, and I would like you to promise that you'll let her be happy and die of old age. I can give you money for her food, and I'm sure your Aunt May can tell you how to raise her, but don't make her go back to Bryant's Farms or end her days with an axe through her neck. Or being strangled." He became agitated again and started to use Ruby's own throat to illustrate how chickens are strangled until she shoved him away.

"Ned, stop!" Ruby said. "I understand and I will keep the chicken. I won't even eat chicken when she's around."

"I've been calling her Sweetie," Ned offered, and then they both saw how the chicken had hopped up onto one of the kitchen chairs and appeared to be reading yesterday's newspaper. "I think she's quite smart."

"She does seem to be," Ruby observed.

"Just tell people that your Aunt May gave her to you and nobody'll be the wiser. Now I doubt Bryant will bother you because I took the backwoods route over here," Ned speculated, lowering his voice again. "The general gossip is that I've been hot after your tail, but you're not falling for my pitch. I'm going to jump the five-thirty redeye train so I'll catch it at the whistle stop just outside of town. That's only another mile or two from here and I'm a fast walker. Will you make me a thermos of your delicious coffee for the road?"

"Of course," Ruby said, filling the percolator with grounds and water and setting it on the stovetop. Then she saw Ned give her a hot after your tail look and she smiled and then they began kissing and straining toward each other while the chicken investigated the sugar bowl.

"Why can't you be more decisive," he muttered, tearing at her dress. "Why can't you just come with me now! At least let's take the last step—I hate leaving all so many things unfinished. We've been together this past week and it's like watching a special magic star form, but we need that top point. Let's put the top peak on that star—please, Ruby, let's go further and *be* with each other."

She was losing this battle and ready to put the top peak on too, and Ned was so close to stardom there by the stove and sink that she almost swooned—until she felt extreme pain and smelled something scorching. In their frenzy, they had moved too close to the range and Ruby's forearm and some of the light brown hairs upon it had gotten scorched by the flame making fresh coffee.

"Ow, *ow!*" she snapped, pulling away. She and Ned examined the burned area and Ned dabbed it with cool water and kissed it, but his lips were much more gentle now and the moment was lost for both of them. She filled the thermos with coffee and poured a cup for herself, and Ned glanced at the kitchen wall clock.

"I suppose I should go," he said. "It'll be at least a half an hour walk."

She had to grab him one last time before he left, just to feel all his steely skinniness and hug him with confused affection.

"Please be careful—in everything you do," she begged. "I don't know that we'll end up together or that I'll ever believe as strongly as you'd like, but I do believe in a great deal of what you stand for and I want you to really leave your mark on the world."

He hugged her tightly back. "All right," he said. "Now I feel like I've accomplished something during this visit. Goodbye, Ruby."

She pulled him back by the collar. "I'm going to worry about your getting safely on the train," she whispered. "And not being clobbered by any of Bryant's goons. Will you let me or your mother know you're okay once you get to New York?"

He narrowed his keen gray eyes. "I'll let you know even sooner," he promised. "Frank runs the dawn train and I'll have him blow the whistle twice when I get on. You should be able to hear it from here. And if you don't hear it, well, then avenge my death."

"Oh, Ned," she sighed, shaking her head.

It was still dark when he snuck away, but soon after the sun peered over the rim of the mountains and pushed its way into full orange and pink splendor. Ruby fed the chicken some dry toast and fresh water and then she heard a double toot from the five-thirty run in the near distance. She smiled when she heard the whistles, yet a part of her felt somewhat hollow to see Ned leave. She hadn't been able to make all the sacrifices of face powder and materialism and sausage links that he'd hoped for, but she did feel a uniquely exhausted gratitude toward Ned's pushing her to new limits, and to his opening her eyes to many things that she had never quite seen before.

Aunt May helped her set up a small coop and taught her the basics of chicken rearing, with Sweetie only laying eating eggs, since there was no rooster around for fertilization yet. Sweetie enjoyed scraps and any kind of bug she could find, and she was amiable and fond of being petted or talked to. She gave a satisfied cluck every time she laid an egg, and her output was steady and of good shape and size. Furthermore, when Sweetie kept jumping onto tables and pecking at loose change or bottle caps, Ruby got the idea to see if she'd play checkers. Sweetie was indeed smart enough to learn to peck at the checker pieces without knocking them off the board, but she did have trouble distinguishing between the red and black pieces. Yet who knew what she might learn in time, and she definitely was a chicken who should have been saved from Death and Farmer Bryant's miserable cold hands or axe blade.

Aunt May seemed to be stopping by more often and Ruby wasn't sure whether that was because she wanted to keep a closer eye on the love spell happenings or because she was impressed with Sweetie. Ruby also thought she had seen Aunt May heading toward Henry Gwynn's, but then she realized that Aunt May was probably taking a shortcut into town and maybe just looking around to be sure that Henry was still alive. Somebody had to check in on the poor man sometime, although a reasonably new car was parked at Henry's every now and then—but never for too long.

Once when Aunt May had come by, Ruby asked whether her father had liked hanging around the kitchen more than the other rooms. She couldn't figure out why the kitchen seemed to be such a romantic hotbox wherein she had received marriage proposals from Ben and Ned and some heightened prospective attention from Eli as well. Aunt May said that while her father had preferred the front room by the woodstove and the bookcase, her grandparents had made the kitchen their own special spot and were always nuzzling like a pair of turtledoves.

"Worse than Alma and Jasper even," she noted.

"My, that's pretty nuzzly," Ruby said, guessing that the turtledoves had left their longing for togetherness behind and that it even radiated through the linoleum sometimes.

When she made her usual weekly trip to the library after Ned's departure, she and Mrs. Whist exchanged meaningful smiles. Ruby was taking out Martha Ostenso's *Wild Geese* and Mrs. Whist asked her to let her know how it was when she was through.

"I haven't gotten around to reading it yet," Mrs. Whist said. "Oh, Ruby, I really wish you could be my daughter-in-law!"

"I wish that too!" Ruby insisted. "But Ned's just—"

"Yes, yes, I understand," Mrs. Whist sighed.

"He's so socially conscious and forward-thinking," Ruby continued. "And he's cute as a cat and I love his voice, which is important because he talks constantly. He just can be progressively overwhelming sometimes, though. Not to change the subject," she added, because this matter really had been on her mind lately. "But my father collected lots of books, including first editions and autographed copies, and I was thinking that the Bright Bend Library might need them. I'd like to keep some myself, but I'm sure he would have wanted the bulk of the collection to end up here."

Mrs. Whist regarded her tortoiseshell fountain pen for a moment, then she clapped her hands.

"Why don't we give your father his own honorary reading room?" she suggested excitedly. "We'll consolidate the fiction and biographies and let him have the room with the bay window. Won't that be splendid?"

"Yes, I think it will," Ruby laughed. "And I have an honest to goodness portrait of him that can hang on the wall. Like he's Woodrow Wilson or something."

"We can use Ned's antique globe," Mrs. Whist added. "His grandfather gave it to him and it's so impressive and large. Ned feels that the globe is elitist and imperialist, though, so he won't mind. And Ben Greenlee made a golden oak table for the library a few years ago when he was trying to impress my predecessor Jenny Walsh, but we were never sure what to do with it and it's in the basement now. It's a fine piece of carving and I think your father's reading room would be the perfect place."

Table from Ben, portrait from Eli, globe from Ned—now that would also make it the Andrew J. Pritchard's Daughter's Summer Suitors Room, Ruby thought, but then again who really needed to hear about all that.

The dearest wife can endure shared sufferings. Grasp a nettle firmly to quietly suffer its sting and know that your pain will bring a noble love to you.

V.

❁

It was beyond hot. It was steaming and blistering and broiling and Ruby never could seem to draw in a decent breath of air, and if a breeze did manage to stir itself up it was quickly flattened by the sheer effort of penetrating an August scorcher. She could feel heat seeped into the crooks of her elbows and knees, along the nape of her neck, under bed sheets. The ground was starting to crack and split, tree leaves were wilted and every garden plant and wildflower was bent downward in desperate green prayers for rain. Ruby hiked to Oval Lake hoping for a few degrees of relief and some swimming, but the water was sluggish and slimy with algae clogging the shoreline, so very different than when Ruby had been there just weeks earlier with Ned Whist.

Ruby felt sluggish and crabby and full of algae herself. She missed Ned, she missed Ben, she even missed that rascal Eli a little—yet at the same time she resented having met them and wasting her summer in a dump like Bright Bend, and doing this stupid, stupid spell. Just that morning she had had to find a nettle plant and deliberately grab it, so that all the burning needles stung her palm and fingertips until she yelled in anger and pain. This was to prove endurance and tolerance, which truly great love seemed to require. Nothing like gripping a fiery plant when the weather was already fiery enough; Ruby had not suffered quietly, however, and had let loose of a string of salty sailor words that she hadn't even known she'd known herself. Her hand had swelled up afterward and there were all kinds of unnerving red streaks on her wrist, but Aunt May was able to soothe things a bit with one of her compresses and some crushed lavender and lemon balm ground into a moist paste.

"You're a tough one," she appraised, deftly massaging Ruby's wrist and knuckles. "I never had to go this far in the spell, and neither did Alma and neither did your Grandma Ruby, or our sisters Opal and Beryl, or my cousin June, or June's daughters Esther and Hester, and not her granddaughters Glory or Hope either. Now my third cousin Sarah Sue—she did have to run the gauntlet. But the husband she ended up with was a gem—he could play the fiddle and dance and had the most kindly smile—and he wasn't all music and charm either, because he worked for the railroad and built her a big house with cupola on top, you know, one of those rooftop rooms with windows in all four directions." She pronounced *cupola* with careful uncertainty, then pointed her fingers north, south, east and west for emphasis.

Ruby was still irked. "Imagine having to grab a nettle and suffer on purpose," she muttered. "You'd never see any spell making men do things like this."

"Men and women suffer in different ways," Aunt May said, taking some leftover sprigs of lemon balm and adding water, lavender syrup, honey and shaved iced and producing a surprisingly delicious beverage which also managed to cool Ruby down in both body and mind. Ruby waited for Aunt May to explain the difference in the ways in how men and women suffer, but Aunt May went to hang two baskets of laundry instead, pinning the clothes onto long lines of rope stretching from her porch post to a stout tree. Ruby watched in a peevish daze at first, then got up guiltily to help.

"Never mind, dear, I'm fine," Aunt May said, though Ruby insisted and hung her share of freshly-washed sheets, pillowcases and towels, along with Aunt May's cotton nightgowns and carefully stitched underthings. The clothes smelled clean and soapy and seemed dazzling white in the sun.

"I wanted to get them up before it rains later today," Aunt May added. "There's going to be a storm this evening. My wrists are aching plenty."

It was accepted knowledge that Aunt May's wrists ached when a thunderstorm was coming, and if a blizzard was on the way she would feel a tingling in her right elbow. She was never wrong and a few years ago a pair of scientist-types from Penn State had paid her a visit and asked her many questions about her bodily weather predictions. They had heard about them through word of mouth and later wrote them up in a scholarly paper; they had even sent Aunt May a copy of the publication, but Aunt May had found it dull reading and complained that those scientists had taken all of the "heaven and earth" out of her gifts from above.

After the nettle encounter, Ruby headed back home while Aunt May went to her weekly quilting meeting. Just how Ruby's wedding quilt was progressing was not a topic of discussion, and Ruby figured that if Aunt May didn't raise the topic, she wouldn't either. Seeing Aunt May's hand-stitched slips had, however, inspired Ruby to try to hand-sew a chemise out of some cerise silk she'd gotten in New York's Chinatown a couple of years ago, while taking a day trip to Manhattan with Pete. Her hand was still pulsing and hurting, but in a way that forced her to slow her needle and work with more precision. She was halfway done when the late afternoon sun hit the porch like a fireball, however, and her enthusiasm for the project waned. The temperature hadn't budged and there seemed no sign of any storm to bust through the heat yet, and Ruby decided to get more water from the spring down the road while taking a quick shower in it as well.

The spring down the road was in essence a long rusty pipe jutting out of a ledge of rocks, at the point where the road turned hilly and led down into town. Someone had somehow tapped a mountain spring with that pipe, and icy water flowed from it all the time. It offered free refreshment or a cooling spray to passersby, or if you had a well at your house where the water tasted too much like iron or sulfur, you could bring empty milk bottles to the spring and haul back better stuff to drink. Ruby had a sulfury well and made a visit with her milk bottles every other day. She liked the cold vapor that always surrounded the spring and the cushiony patches of moss that grew on the rocks below. This afternoon she stepped right into the rush of water and got herself drenched—she only lived about five minutes away and in weather like this, no one except a few old biddies and the young biddy Annabelle Whist would overly question her being out in public in a soaked dress.

It was a blissful pipe-spring bath and she went back for a second dousing until she was really too cold and her body began to feel strange, being so chilly with so much heat all around. There was also a man coming up the road from town, probably having gotten off the four p.m. train. She still didn't care if her neighbors saw her drenched, but from what she could tell, this man was wearing a sharp linen suit and he had a fast, citified walk, so he was most likely a visiting out-of-towner. Or worse yet a salesman who'd try to start pushing waffle irons or hedge clippers or health tonics on her— salesmen were always trolling around these parts.

She padded home quickly with wet bare feet and dripping hair, her dress bunched between her legs but otherwise refreshed, and after she had put the bottles filled with fresh water in the icebox she went to change into dry things. Until there was a knock at the front door, and she glimpsed the toffee-colored summer suit standing on the porch and rolled her eyes at the thought of listening to another salesman marinated in hair tonic. She went to give him the brush-off, but then she saw that he had a very familiar piano-playing face.

"Pete?" she asked incredulously. "How did you find me?"

Pete gave her a stern look with a great deal of focus on her abdomen. "Your landlady told me what town you'd gone to because she'd seen it on an envelope someone sent. Then when I got here I just kept tossing out questions and people kept answering and pointing the way."

"Gladys the nosy lush, of course," Ruby scoffed. "What'd you have to do? Buy her one beer and she talked?"

"No, I had to buy her *two* beers and she blabbed because she's as concerned about your condition as I happen to be," Pete said, walking into the house and closing the door behind him. "Ruby, are you pregnant? Because I know you don't look it yet, but then it wouldn't have been that long—and why the hell else would you have skipped off without a word to live up here in the sticks? Unless it's because you've gone crackers and had to come here to spend your days dancing around pipe waterfalls—I *knew* that was you when I was walking up the road. Now if you're going to have a kid, don't sweat it—I'm ready to step up to the altar. Don't be afraid to tell me, I've accepted the idea and we'll get hitched as soon as possible. If there's a justice of the peace around we can go right now, but first you'd better fix yourself up and come back onto dry land, mermaid."

Good old crazy Pete. He looked quite nice in his suit and hat, but then he always had a way of looking nice in whatever he happened to be wearing. He had his usual summer tan and his dark hair was sleekly combed and parted; his eyes were angry now but still appealingly big and brown, and he even smelled like the Florida Water Ruby had given him for Christmas. And while it was a kick to watch him spinning around like a top, she ended the baby panic.

"You're sure?" he exacted.

"Yes."

"Then what the hell?" he complained, glancing around irritably at the house and the landscape beyond and all the things that had taken her away from him and his seesawing moods and drunken weekends and chronic inability to be anywhere on time.

"I had to come here for family reasons," she managed after a moment. Not only because she wasn't allowed to reveal the love spell, she also didn't want to reveal it to him. Pete was unusually superstitious and fascinated by things like spells and evil eyes and lucky charms and rituals. So much so that he could not play the piano publicly without taking three chews off a stick of clove gum, then carefully wadding up the rest in his pocket. If he chewed more than three times or had to substitute a different flavor, his playing would be off, and if he didn't chew at all, then the earth would surely be knocked from its orbit and civilization would end. In other words, he always performed some kind of gum-chewing rite and had since his audition to become part of Sunny Bill and His Moonbeams. To tell Pete about any love spell would fill him with awe, curiosity and perverse determination to be the man Ruby ended up with, and therefore it was best to keep doubly quiet on the subject.

"What family reasons?" he persisted, crowding her into the corner by the potted fern. She edged her way free from the fronds.

"Personal reasons," she said. "I can't go into detail now."

"Why, here I'm your boyfriend and we have danced very close—if you happen to recall—and you've eaten Sunday dinner at my mother's table and not every girl I've known has done that, but you can't tell *me*?" he sputtered. "You're a pain in the seat."

"And you're a crank," she sighed. "And by the way, if you haven't noticed there's a huge storm brewing behind you and the sky's starting to turn black."

The storm had begun to roll in, with winds whipping up suddenly and low rumbles of thunder. Ruby hurried outside and hustled Sweetie into her coop while Pete watched, laughing despite his present state of prideful indignation.

"Did you just go get a real chicken and pick her up like a pet?" he asked.

"She is a pet and don't even think about eating her," Ruby warned, giving her usual Sweetie spiel. "Anyone who kills her will be under a terrible curse for the rest of their lives. She comes from a special hexed breed of chickens that are for laying eggs only."

Rather than wondering how chickens could be hexed and by whom, Pete accepted this information solemnly and Ruby guessed that he wouldn't be eating any poultry at all until he was at least fifty miles out of the area. She and Pete then battened down the hatches and prepared for the worst, which came in the form of even wilder directionless wind, the sky turning from black to greenish-black, with whip-like streaks of lightning and more thunder that rattled the glass panes in the windows. Hail followed, pinging and bouncing in hard white pellets, then the electric and phone lines were knocked out—which didn't surprise or trouble Ruby too much, since one of them seemed to go dead every week even in the clearest weather.

Pete was handling the onslaught fairly well, but then he too had grown up in Philadelphia and experienced more than his share of summer heat and raging storms that scared police horses and flooded the streets within minutes. Now he just smoked a cigarette anxiously and peered out at the chaos from behind the curtains, making the sign of the cross after a spectacular hit of lightning that arched and bounced off Mr. Gwynn's outhouse. Ruby watched along with concern, afraid that the stinky rickety building might burst into flames, but it held together and remained upright as it had for many years.

"Sheesh, close call," Pete said.

"Real close," Ruby agreed. "I'm surprised old Henry didn't come running out with his union suit half-down. He's practically always in there doing his business."

"No! That's not a crapper, is it?" Pete asked disgustedly. "Please tell me you have an indoor toilet, Ruby. I know we're out in the country and you're barefoot with chickens running around, but it is 1929, for Christ's sake. People shouldn't still be crapping outside."

"Not me—I have a brand new porcelain toilet, sink and tub," Ruby laughed. "My cousin Alma and her husband Jasper had them put in and they're absolutely beautiful. Feel free to use any or all of them."

"Well, lah-dee, I might just do that, Princess," Pete joked back. "Good to see how even though you're out here with the hill-jacks now, you've got better plumbing than you have in Philly. Like that cold water faucet in your bathroom sink that never turns all the way off. It's like listening to a babbling brook day and night, if you can tune out that frog-voiced newspaper kid on the corner and the streetcars running every ten minutes."

Ruby smiled, remembering those passing trolleys and the croaky newspaper boy and the trickling faucet and some fun times with Pete—yet then she also remembered other not so fun moments like waiting for him to show up when he was hours late or tiptoeing around him while he slept off an all-nighter on the couch. How he could be selfish in the sack, or how he ate up all the food in the icebox and left cigarette stubs everywhere. But then he could be so affectionate and caring, or carrying in bags full of delicatessen treats or champagne and flowers. You never knew what you were going to get with Pete, whether it would be the King of Hearts or the Joker. And just when you grew used to one card—when you were completely in love or completely fed up—the other would show its face and utterly confuse you.

Which was why she had taken off to Bright Bend in the first place, to escape the either/or scenario and hope for something better. Ruby had realized that she had gotten into a rut of tolerating Pete by loving or hating him and that she was amazingly pretty good at all that, but it still didn't seem right. There just had to be more—or something of a middle ground. Of course she hadn't found any middle ground or even a neutral park bench here, and she was starting to think that maybe it was all her fault and maybe she really was a pain in the seat like Pete had said. But it was probably best to finish the goofy magic summer and see what transpired and who came out of the vapory clouds—if anyone—before passing judgment on herself. Besides, maybe Pete was the Love Spell Lover and her taking off had knocked a cup of sense into him. She had a gut feeling that that wasn't the case, but she allowed him to kiss her to be sure and for old times' sake, though she did stop his hands from venturing toward formerly familiar turf.

"What?" he objected, moving his mouth across her now-exposed collarbone. "It's you, it's me—it's us. Nothing wrong with that."

The storm had turned to a lulling rain, pattering onto the roof and running in rivulets down the windows. A softly rushing rain, like how the water tap in her apartment had always softly flowed in the background while she and Pete were together; it would be so easy to be together now, to just let him continue and to enjoy it all herself. He had taken a train to find her, he had made such an effort—and he seemed so glad to be with her now. It would be so easy to let things keep going—but no, it would be too easy, and too many steps backward. She managed to wriggle out from under him and slide off the couch.

"What?" he said again, smoothing back his hair then removing his suit jacket and draping it neatly over the chair by the desk. This was a surprise, since Pete would normally have tossed the jacket to wherever it might land, and Ruby wasn't sure if this was due to him turning over a new leaf or just being the owner of a new suit and not wanting it to get wrinkled. "What's wrong? Why are you looking at me like I have two heads?" he complained.

"Because you do have two heads," Ruby laughed, mussing up the hair he had just fixed. "Another one popped out a few minutes ago and it's even handsomer than your original."

"Then get over here and kiss them both," he urged, patting the couch cushion beside him, but Ruby shook her own head firmly no. "Oh, why not," Pete sighed. "What's curdling your cream lately?"

"It doesn't work anymore, Pete," she answered frankly. "It's all so slapdash and here now, gone later."

"But you never cared about that in the past," he insisted. "Or never enough to leave or break things off."

"Maybe I didn't before, but there's too much past now," she said. "It's been five years and I just want more."

"Like a ring and a promise," he muttered. "You girls are all alike. I thought you were different, Ruby, but you're singing the usual tune."

"No, it's not so much about rings and promises, just fondness and togetherness and willingness too." She straightened his hair again for him, then traced her finger down the sharp curves of his profile. "I very much appreciate your wanting to get married because you thought I was pregnant, but that's no way to start things off. Marriage shouldn't be forced."

He grinned. "Don't be loopy—half the marriages in the world are forced because a girl's knocked-up and most of them work out all right. It's like Fate gives you a swift kick in the ass forward, that's all. Lots of times it's because the woman set a trap herself to force the guy into action, but any guy who's getting some tail has to take that risk."

"What a touchingly romantic description. And you can't ever accuse me of that," Ruby reminded. She was rather fanatical about birth control methods where Pete was concerned, not wanting to set traps or worry and pray every month.

"I wouldn't ever accuse you in the least," he amended seriously. "You're a straight shooter and you always have been. I know I'm no cakewalk and I do love you for hanging in there, Ruby." His eyes filled briefly with tears and then so did hers, but neither of them cried. "And if you want to get married, I guess we still can. No, we still can—and we should, right?"

"We shouldn't," she whispered, and while Pete looked solemnly at the floor, he didn't provide much argument. "You're not there yet. That's not to say that you'll never be there, because I think eventually you'll love having your own family and house with a piano in the living room and a big garden out back. You just have more road touring to do, Pete. Even though you're not on the road as much anymore with the Moonbeams, you're still traveling. Does that make sense?"

"It makes too much sense," he said flatly, getting up and lighting another cigarette. "But don't close the casket yet. I might just kick myself in the pants and take action."

"I could kick you too, for real and with my foot and all, if you think that might help," Ruby offered, and Pete said that he'd keep that in mind.

"What's this?" he asked, fingering the silk chemise that Ruby had started. "It's pretty."

"Just some sewing I was doing before you got here." Despite the indeed too strange coincidence of fashioning a camisole out of the red silk she had bought in Chinatown with Pete and then having him show up hours later— like she had stitched him *toward* her with a needle and thread—Ruby kept mum. Pete didn't handle fluky things very well and, like learning about the love spell, it would make him superstitiously determined to stick around. "How long are you here for?" she asked.

He shrugged, still fingering the silk absently. Not because he remembered her buying it, Ruby was sure, it was just that he liked silky fabrics and bright colors. "The band's scheduled to play one of the resorts upstate at the end of the week, so I told them I'd go on ahead myself to try to find you, then catch up with them later. I didn't know if we'd be tying the knot right off or if you'd even let me in the door. Say, are you planning to wear this red-hot little item up here and if so, who for? Is some other dope in the picture?"

"I only have as many dopes in my picture as you do in yours," Ruby countered, while Pete now pretended to examine her velvet pincushion.

"You know, if you weren't such a wiseass and were more gentle and giving, I might settle down," he muttered.

"Oh, will you please can it!" Ruby flared back. "If I were more gentle and giving I would have jumped off a roof by now. Or stuck my head in the oven. How do you think gentle and giving women feel when they make candlelit dinners for a man who decides to go to an all-night poker game instead without letting them know? Or when they have to run down to the police station to bail out their dreamboat for getting his face punched in in a drunken brawl? Or when some total stranger of a woman accosts them in Woolworth's and introduces herself as the mother of your child!"

"That was *by no means* my kid and we discussed that and you said we wouldn't ever speak of it again," Pete replied tersely.

"I'll speak of it when you start criticizing me for having an inch of backbone and lip!" she yelled, feeling like she might pop a vein from so much righteous indignation until she realized something else and smiled. For the first time since that morning, all the pain and heat from the nettle incident was gone. The redness had vanished as well and her fingers were limber again.

"What is it?" he asked nervously. "What's made you so happy all of a sudden?"

"I ran across a nettle plant this morning," she explained, not going into further detail. "They're awful things and they'll burn up any skin they touch, but just now when we were fighting, the whole part of my hand that grabbed the nettle stopped hurting. It's almost like I got hotter than the pain itself, so it evaporated."

"That's great," Pete said. "I hate to think you were hurting from a stupid plant—and see, I am worth having around every once in a while. And you really do smile so sweet. You should smile more often, Ruby."

She nodded. "Then you should make me smile more often, Pete, instead of making me want to brain you with a lamp."

"Right," he noted. "That might help."

They reached a temporary truce and agreed that Ruby should put on clothes that weren't damp and clammy and then they should eat dinner.

"Where's the best chow around?" Pete asked. "Let's do some fine dining—I've got a fat enough bankroll."

"The best place is the dining parlor at the boardinghouse but you won't like the food," Ruby predicted. "It's the best place around here but it can't hold a candle to what we're used to in the city. If you had a car we might have more options, but even then with the roads so muddy from the storm it'd be quite a production to get anywhere."

"So what's in your pantry?" he prompted. "What can we rustle up ourselves? I know we can't eat Chicken Little outside but let's take a look otherwise."

Raiding of the pantry was stopped, however, by Alma's arrival. Alma had an umbrella and was wearing rain boots, and she instantly guessed who Pete was and welcomed him.

"Everyone's phones are dead so I figured I'd stroll over and see how you were doing. I also heard about the mysterious traveler who was looking for Ruby earlier!" she exclaimed.

"We don't necessarily need telephones around here," Ruby advised Pete. "Not with Hazel in the post office and Vernon at the train station. They're like my landlady Gladys in Philadelphia, but not as shifty."

"Please come over for supper," Alma urged. "We have a piano for Pete to play, and I've got lots of cold roast pork and an asparagus soufflé. With homemade peach ice cream for dessert."

"I'm sold," Pete said, grabbing his jacket and hat. Ruby hurried to put on another dress and her fringed shawl as well, because it was awfully pretty and Pete had given it to her for her birthday and it was nice to dandy up every now and then.

They had to rush back to Alma's because Jasper tended to fret if his supper was late.

"We've got company, Jasp!" Alma announced as they burst through the door. "Ruby and Mr. Pete Nickels of Sunny Bill and His Moonbeams." She wrenched off her boots and dropped them in the foyer. "They looked like a couple of movie stars on the way here with the Morton Salt girl tagging behind them."

Jasper looked Pete over with his usual shrewd friendliness, then he became host-like and offered cigarettes and lemonade. Ruby heard them discussing baseball and automobiles after a few minutes as she helped Alma lay out the food, although Alma brought out the good china for this occasion since they were entertaining a "celebrity." She also had Ruby pick and shake the rain off a few peonies from the garden, then placed them in a crystal dish at the center of the table.

"Wow, some spread," Pete appraised.

"Alma is a wonder," Jasper concurred, carefully removing a half-drowned inchworm from a peony petal and flicking it back into the yard.

"Pete, you would never have gotten such a delicious meal at the boardinghouse," Ruby added. "Alma's an excellent cook."

"Now all of you stop," Alma objected. "Or at least start writing these compliments down so I can put them in my scrapbook. Incidentally, Ruby, you're no slouch in the kitchen yourself."

"Eh," Ruby said. "I get by."

"You get more than by," Pete argued. "My ma taught her to make spaghetti sauce and some other family recipes, and don't tell my mother this because she's a perfect saint of a woman, but I swear Ruby makes better meatballs." He paused to cross himself furtively, out of guilty love for the sainted one. "I feel bad saying it but it's true."

Since it was already past his regular dinnertime, Jasper was at the head of the table reaching for the cold pork roast. He beckoned for everyone to join him. "Please, let's eat before I start getting surly. And Pete, Alma's pumpkin pie is much, much better than that of my dear departed mother, but I of course never could tell Mother and I still don't feel quite right saying it now." He lowered his voice. "She might be listening. She was always something of an eavesdropper in her day."

After dinner and the promised peach ice cream, the inevitable meeting of Pete and piano occurred—and that was how it went for about four more hours. Alma considered him live entertainment and Jasper soon came to the same conclusion, and while Ruby had been through all this before, she enjoyed watching how happy Alma was to listen to her ivories being tickled expertly and how happy Pete was to be made a fuss over. Pete incidentally chewed his clove gum thrice before starting up, which meant he considered this a public performance and was anxious about impressing his audience.

He went through the standards, then he went through the classical and operatic pieces he had learned from Mrs. Biasetti in her tiny studio on 10th Street. Then he started the dance numbers and Alma of course had to dance, or she had to sit by Pete on the piano bench and let him encourage her to play along. And when Alma was working the keys instead of the floorboards, Jasper dragged Ruby up to dance instead, which was no chore because Jasper was light on his feet and an ace rug cutter. Pete had gotten Alma to speed up her notes and gain confidence, and she did an excellent job on the *Tiger Rag* all by herself while Pete took a cigarette break and turned music pages.

"Goodness!" she marveled when she was through with the song. "It was like someone else was playing!"

"Careful, kitty," Jasper warned, patting the top of her head. "We don't want you running off to work in one of those honky-tonks."

Alma turned around and gave Jasper many kisses of furious reassurance. "Never, never—I'd never leave my Jasp for anything!"

Pete smirked at Ruby. "Is that what you're looking for?" he murmured in her ear. "To be like Jack and Jill there?"

"Well, kind of," she whispered. "Not quite so bad, but they do have a special love."

"What's wrong, Pete?" Alma fretted. "Are we boring you? Have you had enough piano for tonight? Would you like a cocktail maybe? Jasper, why don't we fix some whiskey and ginger ales with maraschino cherries?"

"I'll take that offer and I don't even need a cherry," Pete said, while Ruby sat up in shock.

"A cocktail!" she burst out. "With real alcohol? Here I've been hanging around these two for months and I've gotten nothing stronger than lemonade, but Pete comes along for one night and turns their house into a speakeasy."

"All libations have their moment," Jasper said, revealing that a secret stash was kept behind the Victrola records.

After the whiskey arrived, the laughter became louder and a few off-color jokes emerged from Pete and even Jasper, and ultimately Alma and Jasper danced their way upstairs for a private rendezvous. Once they were gone, Pete polished off what was left of the second bottle, with a few slugs of the blackberry brandy also in Jasper's stash for good measure. Not surprisingly, he soon became amorous as well.

"Let's go back to your house," he urged Ruby, pulling her close. "And take a bath in that nice new white tub."

"No baths for us," Ruby said, guiding Pete toward Alma and Jasper's spare bedroom, which was where Alma, Jasper, and all of Bright Bend would expect Pete to sleep. Ruby detailed this moral code to Pete, who found it tiresome and kept trying to steer her onto the spare bedroom mattress, but fortunately by this point Pete was more tired than lusty and settled for hitting the mattress by himself. Ruby helped him off with his shirt and pants, shoes and socks and sock garters, leaving him contentedly in his underwear draped beneath a modest sheet. For old times sake she brought a glass of ice water in and left it on the bureau, because Pete often woke up thirsty after boozing, but after that she slipped quietly out. The walk home was peaceful and somewhat foggy, a haze of mist rising from the wet ground and crickets trilling in the dark. Ruby had had plenty of libations herself and was glad to call it a night, covering herself with her own modest bed sheet and still hearing strains of the *Tiger Rag* as she drifted off into whiskey and ginger ale dreamland.

In the morning, Ruby woke early enough to bake some blueberry and lemon muffins and bring them over to Alma and Jasper's for breakfast. She expected Alma and Jasper to be bustling about as usual, getting ready to trot over to the pharmacy, while Pete would still be asleep. Instead, Alma and Jasper were a shade hung-over and sluggish and confessed to having each drunk a Bromo to clear their heads and consciences. Pete on the other hand was dressed and amiably drinking coffee while glancing at the Binghamton paper; he had even showered, shaved with the guest razor, combed his hair and put on a clean shirt.

"Never try to match drinks with Pete," Ruby said. "You've heard of dance marathons? He could enter drinking marathons. Don't expect him to show any effects from last night because that was all just like a little nightcap for him, right?"

Pete nodded. "Between that and this mountain air, I was out like a log. Best sleep I've had in years."

Though she was bleary, Alma had nonetheless managed to make more coffee, squeeze fresh orange juice and poach half a dozen eggs. She was weakly excited to see Ruby's muffin basket, however, because she was running low on bread. Pete tore into the muffins and the rest of the food eagerly, while Alma and Jasper forced down some black coffee and toast wedges.

"Mm-mmm," Pete said. "You girls are top-notch cooks. And Ruby, I really wish I could stick around until you get sick of me but I just got a telegram from the band. I told Sunny Bill that I'd be here, of course, and you sure weren't kidding that the rest of this town knows everybody's business. They had that telegram delivered by seven a.m. We're still playing that resort job but we've got a last minute show in Atlantic City before then, so I'll have to head back this morning and hitch a ride with the boys. If you'd like to hop the train with me and come to Philly for a while too, I'd love the company."

Alma and Jasper both sobered up a bit more, waiting for Ruby's reply. Ruby poured everyone another round of coffee.

"I think I'll stay here through the summer at least," she said. "To finish up that personal business I mentioned before. But you're always welcome to visit again, Pete."

"Don't think I won't do that, Kewpie doll," Pete insisted, giving her cheek a pinch. "This was a lot more laughs than I expected."

"Pete, speaking for Kewpie and Alma and myself, we'd love to see you return," Jasper noted. "But next time we drink gin," he said. "Gin doesn't fill my noggin up with concrete or flip my stomach inside out. I'm not cut from the same cloth as you, my friend—one more whiskey evening like this and I'll end up in the hospital."

They all went to the station so that Pete could catch the 9:03 bound for Philadelphia, though Jasper left before the train arrived because he had to get busy with his usual vials and powders and mortars and pestles. The train snorted in right on time and the conductor stepped off, snapped open his watch and announced that they would be leaving in eight minutes. Pete gave

Alma a friendly parting hug and kiss, and then Alma went over to chitchat with Vernon in the stationhouse and to give Pete and Ruby some privacy.

"Jump on the train with me," Pete said, pretending to try to drag her aboard. "Really. Come with me and we'll get married in Atlantic City. It'll be fun."

"It'll be fun for about a week until you realize you're an honest to God husband," Ruby predicted.

"I might not," he frowned back. "You're so no-nonsense, Ruby Jane. Just take a leap."

"You'd better take a leap onto this train, Peter Dominic, since there won't be another one for hours," Ruby said. She smoothed his suit jacket lapels and gave him a long kiss, which like all of her kisses with Pete had her leaning in towards his warmth and charm, but this time it felt like it had some finality to it. Or at least she felt the finality.

Pete went for another kiss of his own then bounded onto the train, but he hung around the door area waving until the conductor prodded him back toward the seats. Pete was still waving when they pulled away, and he called from the window that he'd see her at the end of the summer and to wear her red shimmy. Ruby shook her head, wondering how long it would take for this parting scene to work its way around town. Alma sidled up beside her, smiling.

"He's a handful," Alma assessed. "Though maybe worth it. You know the best horses are the ones you have to break in."

"Yes, your husband's one of the best and he was such a hellion, wasn't he?" Ruby joked.

"Oh, shush," Alma said. "Maybe I personally didn't have to break in anyone but I've seen it happen with other women. But then some others did just get thrown into a ditch and the horses left them for dead," she reasoned further. "It's probably six of one, half a dozen of another."

Ruby held out her right hand, showing Alma how all the nettle marks had disappeared. "That nettle was to teach me tolerance and patience, but it's only been since I've stopped having tolerance and patience for Pete that he's started to make more effort."

"Because he needs a challenge," Alma suggested. "He's one of those types."

"But I don't always want a challenge, or to be challenging," Ruby sighed. "And yesterday before you showed up Pete and I were having a big fight, and I was really laying into him and suddenly I noticed how all the pain from the nettle went away. Like I was rewarded for losing my temper! I swear I keep finding other meanings for everything in this spell—isn't that crazy?"

"No, it just seems like you're creating your own magic and making the spell your own," Alma said. "Now tell me what magic you used on Pete's mother's meatballs and sauce recipe to make that your own. Secret spice? Dash of sugar?"

"I only drained the grease from the meatballs after frying," Ruby demurred. "Pete's mother leaves it in. That makes the sauce heavier."

Alma squinted at her skeptically. "Nothing else?"

Ruby smiled. "I might have added a quarter teaspoon of cinnamon too. It sweetens the tomatoes and also tastes good with the ground beef."

"I knew there had to be something!" Alma whooped. "Will you make that for me and Jasp? In your red shimmy?"

Ruby laughed. "Only if you and Jasp will polish off another batch of cocktails and dance the hootchie-koo."

Alma smirked. "Anytime. And maybe Pete will be joining us again."

"Or maybe he won't."

"You know, there's not much left to August and summer'll be wrapping up soon," Alma noted. "It's not like you have oodles of days to work with. Pete's surprise appearance was pretty interesting, you have to admit."

"I refuse to answer on the grounds that I don't want to," Ruby said, and then she and Alma strolled over to the pharmacy to see how Jasper and his morning-after memories were holding up.

Not too long after Pete's visit, Ruby went to the county fair with Jasper, since Aunt May was off bringing supper to someone she just referred to cryptically as a "shut-in" and Alma wasn't feeling well.

"She's queasy and clammy," Jasper said. "She kept insisting on trying a recipe for steak tartare the other night and I don't believe it was the wisest venture. I didn't eat a bite because you do realize that involves *raw* meat and eggs together? And now she's sadly paying the price for being a sophisticate."

The county fair was a contented gathering of people from all over the region wandering about playing games of chance or eating fudge, caramel apples, cotton candy, scrapple, hot dogs, divinity, taffy, peanut brittle or hand-dipped chocolates—or in the case of a few small boys who had just been on the Ferris Wheel too long, upchucking all of the featured treats into the high grass by the Fair's entrance. There was a unique smell of spun sugar, collective tobaccos and dusting powders, sizzling grease and manure from the different livestock on display. Ruby took a look at the prize chickens and felt that Sweetie was as worthy as any of them, and she smiled at Aunt May's Sapphire Star quilt, which had many admirers and had earned a blue ribbon. She exchanged pleasantries with Hazel from the post office and Lewis Tyler and

Mrs. Whist who were over by the Philco Radio tent, and she glimpsed a tall, dark and handsome-enough man she had seen in Royal Bend now judging the pie contest along with the mustachioed Athena Sweet Shop owner. And then Ruby was beckoned to elaborately by the gypsy fortuneteller.

"I can read your future," boasted the woman, who wore a Bombay gold turban, Chinese satin slippers, a Japanese kimono, about a hundred bangle bracelets and if Ruby wasn't mistaken, a hint of Emeraude perfume. "I see a love from a faraway and exotic land. Look for him soon."

Though she claimed to be able to foretell more, Ruby declined; she only wanted to invest a buck in this oracle and was also worried that she might receive bad news. Jasper was waiting for her outside the fortuneteller's booth, finishing a disk of scrapple wrapped in wax paper.

"I only eat this once a year at the Fair," he noted. "Never have a taste for it otherwise but can't get enough of it here. Never get sick from it either, like my darling wife and her steak tartare. So what went on with Madame Zamorova?"

Ruby recounted her gypsy prediction.

"My heavens, a faraway and exotic land—sounds like a fellow from Milwaukee to me," Jasper laughed.

"Do you think she means Pete?" Ruby wondered. "He's about as foreign as exotic as anyone I've ever known."

"I think she says the same thing to every other person," Jasper suggested soundly. "She tells you to look for a foreign prince, she tells another girl that love is closer than she thinks, she tells older women that lost loves are going to return, she tells us men either to expect trouble in business or much prosperity—and yammer yammer give me a dollar, please."

"I suppose you're right," Ruby said. "Wow, Jasper, people sure are flapping away with your fans," she pointed out.

Jasper had arranged to have hundreds of mint green paper fans on wooden sticks ready for the Fair, with an advertisement for the Bright Bend Pharmacy on one side and a tawny-haired round-cheeked picture-of-health girl on the other. It was a sticky night, so the fans were in high demand. Jasper watched and exulted from the sidelines at his fluttering success, and then he dragged Ruby off to the scrapple stand, insistent that she share in his annual joy over the thrifty combination of pork scraps, herbs, black pepper and cornmeal, always best eaten amid the bright lights and sounds of a Fair—and with a dash of ketchup, mustard or apple jelly.

Into a tub as hot as you can bear, drop a bowlful of the summer's last rose petals and bathe until you are clean and fragrant. Place one whole bloom by your easternmost window and know that as the sun rises beyond it, your true love will arrive by sunset of the same day.

VI.

❀

With the last day of summer closing in and no results from the spell, Ruby gave Aunt May a sadly smug smile.

"What did I tell you?" she sighed. "I knew it wouldn't work. Has anybody tried this since women got the vote? Maybe all that emancipation made old-timey magic unnecessary. Maybe we should just start taking even more steps forward and order husbands out of the Sears catalog. That way we can get the right height, weight, religion, personality—and buy a new toaster at the same time."

She swatted one big fat fly away, then another. They were over by Aunt May's fly-happy compost heap full of potato peels, apple cores, eggshells and coffee grounds, all sloppily enriching a heap of soil. This soil was then mixed in with garden earth, with the results being Aunt May's gorgeous vegetables and heady roses you could smell ten feet away. Aunt May was picking at some of her red and pink beauties now, meticulously pulling off select petals and placing them in a bowl.

"Here," she said to Ruby, handing her the bowl when it was nearly full. "It's the last part of the spell—which isn't over yet, young lady, not until summer's final minute. And how it's ever going to succeed with you always thinking that it won't is another thing."

Ruby took the bowl then reached up to balance it on top of her head. "What now, Auntie? Walk a mile without dropping it? Or throw all the petals off a cliff then jump right after them?"

"I'll throw you off a cliff soon enough," Aunt May laughed. "You and your father with your smart mouths. And listen up, this is all you've got left to do—take your petals and draw a bath with water as hot as you can stand it. In fact, the hotter the better." She reached back toward the bush and cut off one last red bloom, stem and all. "Add the petals, then steep in the water until you're good and steamed. After that, put this whole rose in a vase or glass by any window facing east, and as the sun rises, it'll bring you your love by sunset."

"By sunset!" Ruby burst out. "You mean by tomorrow some perfect man is going to materialize? That's one big screaming promise, May Belle Campbell."

"He'll be perfect for you," Aunt May exacted. "Whether other people find him perfect is another matter." Ruby smiled. "Is your sweetheart Ben Greenlee back in town? He tipped you off to that fact and you invented all this rosy-posy business to make it look like fate."

Aunt May twisted up her long silvery hair, which had slipped loose from its pins. "I've given up on you and Ben," she sighed. "You can't sell a mirror to a blind man, so I won't waste words trying to convince you. And while I can't speculate on who it'll be, Ruby, it will be someone if you just stop *doubting*."

"Aunt May, I don't know that I can't doubt," Ruby answered with serious sincerity. "It really seems so far-fetched."

Aunt May lightly touched Ruby's hands, now holding the bowl full of rose petals dubiously before her.

"I know it's hard, dear," Aunt May whispered. "I've seen you struggling. But it's one more day and one little bath to take. So if you can't make yourself believe, how about you just keep quiet on the subject? Then the day after tomorrow, you can talk and complain about how things failed until you're blue in the face and I'm green from listening. Can you manage that for me? Just keep quiet until then?"

Ruby nodded, then still holding the petal bowl before her began heading for home.

After checking the house for Eli, easing into very hot water and turning herself into what felt like a boiled rose, Ruby stepped out of the tub, dried off, then scooped all the drowned petals from the drain. Once the overheated feeling faded, she also felt languid and smooth. She began to wonder whether the need for such an extreme bath temperature was to put the spell user into a state of acceptance, because for the first time since she'd begun this quirky quest three months earlier, an actual thought of possibility pushed its way free. But the thought was less like who or what or how, and more like *I am ready.* Like the rose she had set on the windowsill and like the still-full September moon, she felt a definite readiness now, then she even went so far as to speak the words out loud.

"I am ready," she said and she slept heavily, almost as if she'd been drugged, without any dreams or premonitions. In the morning she noticed how there must have been strong winds during the night, since the temperature was cooler and the sheer white curtains had risen up and thrown a veil over the nearby armchair. The rose had stayed where it was, however, and the glass that held it was now suffused with color as sun filtered through the water and flooded it with light.

Because September 18th would have been her father's birthday, Ruby, Alma and Mrs. Whist had planned a small celebration on the following Saturday at the library to mark the opening of the Andrew J. Pritchard Reading Room. In truth, the room itself was just a long oak table and two glass-doored bookcases, a sideboard with a globe and a green-shaded lamp underneath Eli Turnby's portrait. Anyone who wanted to read and reflect upon Andrew Pritchard and the words and stories he had collected could sit under his image at the table crafted by Ben Greenlee—or perhaps study Ned Whist's globe. If nothing else comes of this spell, Ruby thought, at least it had resulted in some key items for the memorial to Andrew J. And a few rather interesting experiences and acquaintances—and an incredibly smart chicken who might be able to use the Reading Room herself.

She knew that her father would have hated speeches or recollections of his life, so after the unveiling of the portrait—during which the purple velvet drape got stuck and almost knocked the painting down—there was simply a service of coffee and punch, along with finger sandwiches and a showpiece of a cake that Alma had made. Alma had managed to design the cake in the shape of a large open book, with different colored frostings to give the effect of binding and pages along with finely-scrawled lines of text; a work so beautiful that nobody wanted to eat it, until Alma grabbed a knife and cut the first slice for herself.

"Come on now, people," she insisted. "Dig in—it's got raspberry filling!"

Attending were Alma and Jasper, Aunt May and a good showing of people from town, including postmistress Hazel who sat and stared at Ruby's father's portrait and wept heartily into a lace handkerchief—though she was soon diverted by the Book Cake and downed three pieces. Jenny Walsh took the train in from Royal Bend with her baby Charlotte, who seemed to have inherited a respect for books from her mother and behaved angelically for at least an hour, but then wailed like a banshee until Jasper snuck her out in her carriage for a quick walk outside.

Mrs. Whist presided as Official Librarian and tried not to fuss too much over punch cups being left on the table and smudgy fingers touching pages and glass, and Annabelle Whist was there as well, along with Phillip, Annabelle's new beau. Phillip was skittish and snobbish, with Ichabod Crane looks and an affected English accent that traveled back to his home state of Kansas every now and then. Annabelle introduced Phillip as a playwright, but he also edited encyclopedia text and was quite the up-and-comer in that cutthroat field. He spent the afternoon in a corner chair ignoring everyone and gobbling down canapés and cucumber and cream cheese sandwiches, then he complained of having a headache and made Annabelle take him back to Mrs. Whist's house so that Annabelle could fix him an ice pack and a cup of tea with milk and sugar.

"I hope you find yourself a treasure like my Phillip," Annabelle murmured to Ruby upon parting. "Though you'll have to look beyond Bright Bend to do it, of course. Honestly, Ruby, I'd rather see you marry my horrible brother than end up becoming a permanent resident of this silly dot on the map."

"It's beyond belief how much that girl inflates herself. She's like a big blonde hot air balloon," Alma scoffed after Annabelle and Phillip had left. "And I never saw a young man gripe so much about food he couldn't stop eating. Old Phil polished off practically the whole tray of hors d'oeuvres and I think he swallowed some of the sandwich toothpicks as well. But he just kept chewing through them, like a goat."

"The cake's down to crumbs too now," Ruby observed. "Alma, that was the most amazing creation. You should write out the recipe and instructions, because my old magazine *Leisurely and Lively Ladies* would pay some choice bucks for a feature like that. Look at your husband," she then said, laughing at Jasper as he fox-trotted around the room while holding baby Charlotte. "He's kept her entertained all afternoon, and thank God, because that little cherub has quite a set of pipes."

"Don't I know it," Alma said. "I thought she might shatter the glass in the bookcases when she first let loose." Alma then glanced over at Aunt May, who had begun gathering stray napkins and dessert plates and silverware and cleaning up. "Listen, Ruby," she whispered. "I'll tell you this but you need to keep it shushed for a while so it's just between you, me, Jasper, and the lamppost—I think I'm going to have a baby myself."

"What!" Ruby whispered excitedly, gripping Alma's hand.

"I haven't been to the doctor to confirm yet," Alma cautioned. "But I've missed my cycle and I never miss it—I can stand there with a stopwatch and count down to its arrival. I'm too young for the change of life and I've had an upset stomach in the morning and can't stand the sight or smell of butter, and that's *exactly* what my mother went through when she was pregnant with all of us."

"So I'll bet it wasn't even steak tartare that had you sick the other night when Jasper and I went to the Fair," Ruby said.

"No, I doubt it and I will eat that again someday because it was sumptuous. Still, I just about gagged when I was mixing the book cake ingredients this morning and I had to have Jasp step in and cream the butter and sugar and eggs. But don't tell Mom—she'll be heartbroken if I lose the baby or if it's a false alarm." Alma laughed. "Plus I think it'd be such a kick to watch her figure it out herself, as I get bigger and rounder and of course she'll notice how I'll keep running out of the kitchen green-faced every time she puts butter on toast."

Jasper had given Charlotte back to Jenny and fox-trotted alone over to Ruby and Alma. "Looks like you've spilled some beans," he said to his wife. "Did you tell her it's a secret as well?"

"Sure thing, Pops," Alma promised.

"And did you tell her how all this might have happened?" Jasper asked, though he didn't wait for an answer. "Because Mother May there's been trying spells with herbs and hoodoo for years now, but what may have done the trick is when your buddy Pete the piano player was here last month. Remember when we all got stinking on cocktails? That was a romantic night for Alma and myself and I think she and I were so plastered that we just might have had the proper sort of spontaneous combustion."

"Jasper, please," Alma interjected. "Don't embarrass her with too much detail."

"I don't care," Ruby laughed. "And I'll bet he's right, since liquor and music and wild dancing have brought many a child into the world. That combination works for unmarried people all the time."

"We ought to name it Pete, if it's a boy," Alma said. "Or Ruby if it's a girl."

"Or Pete and Ruby if it's twins," Jasper went on. "Or Pete and Ruby and Canadian Whiskey if it's triplets."

"Have quadruplets—or even more if you can squeeze them out," Ruby urged. "If you're going through all that trouble you might as well make it worthwhile."

"Sure, why make one popover when you can cook up half a dozen," Jasper agreed.

"I'll be doing the birthing and I'd prefer just a single seven-pounder," Alma maintained, then she frowned and glanced at the Reading Room entrance.

"Who is that?" she asked, nodding toward a lean, dark-haired man in an olive-colored suit talking to Aunt May. "He looks familiar."

Ruby did a double-take herself. "He does look familiar," she said. "I've seen him twice in Royal Bend and at the county fair too."

"You've seen him in Royal Bend because he's the editor of their *Register*," Jasper detailed. "That's Jeff Bryce—no kin to Fanny Brice, I might add, though he is a witty one. His aunt and uncle run the ice cream place you love so much and he's also a lawyer up there. His mother's Greek and his father was Jefferson Bryce, Sr., one of the best doctors around. Doc Bryce grew up in Royal Bend, married a Greek girl from New York when he was learning to practice medicine, then brought her here. Eventually, her brother and his wife followed and started the Athena Sweet Shop."

"Now I know who he is," Alma said. "He's about our age and was living in Boston, right?"

"Was, until he and his wife stopped walking hand in hand," Jasper corrected. "He moved back to Royal Bend alone about three years ago. "

"Is that so?" Alma said, nudging Ruby with her elbow. "I wonder what brought him to this little confab."

"He's related to Ruby's oddball neighbor Henry Gwynn," Jasper noted further. "He might have been visiting him and stopped by here on his way home. He's one of the few people who Henry lets in the door, and even that's a fairly recent development. I was just talking to Jeff about it at the Twin Bend Civic Board meeting."

The Twin Bend Civic Board had been started earlier in the summer to create good feeling between Royal Bend and Bright Bend, but as Jasper wryly observed every single meeting had been held in Royal Bend and Bright Bend was still being treated like the redheaded stepchild.

"He must be Henry's mysterious guest," Ruby said. "Otherwise no cars ever go near that house. And he must write those quippy things in their paper!" she realized, laughing at her recollection of the most recent one: *Royal Bend has been troubled lately by large numbers of stray dogs and traveling salesmen, and the town therefore plans to train the former to attack the latter on a daily basis.*

Her laughter brought Jefferson Bryce, Jr. over, and he shook Jasper's hand, introduced himself to Alma then pointed a finger at Ruby.

"Why are you always crossing my path?" he asked.

"I don't know, why are you always crossing my path?" she countered, which made him laugh in return.

"Ruby's a fan of your work," Alma said.

"Then I'm a fan of Ruby," he replied.

He was quite all right, Ruby thought, soundly approving of his general person and brown with gray at the temples hair, very straight nose and calm clear green eyes   not too glary or shocking a green, but more like river water after a rain.

Speaking of green, Alma suddenly looked like she might pass out. "Is someone eating butter around here?" she gasped, then Jasper excused them both and guided her out the door as nonchalantly as possible.

"She's not feeling well," Ruby offered. "Summer flu."

"You mean last day of summer flu," Jeff observed and Ruby concurred that yes, summer surely was coming to a close.

After approximately seventeen minutes of additional conversation, Ruby decided that Jeff Bryce was likely the prize in her own enchanted box of Cracker Jack and that she didn't need to fret over the issue anymore. Which was fine, because she had been fretting and wondering and dragonfly hunting all summer and needed a rest—and therefore even if he wasn't the love spell concluder, she was worn out and didn't really care. But in Jeff's case, he was smart, lithe, limber and interestingly attractive, and he also seemed like he might have taken a shine to Ruby as well. He wasn't as obvious as her previous suitors, however, so she wasn't completely sure whether he was just a good flirt or flirting with her. He offered to drive her home because he said he had planned to have supper with his old Cousin Henry anyway, and that he had wanted to check in on the Reading Room ceremony beforehand.

"I never met your father but I've heard a great deal about him," he said. "As a fellow lawyer and someone with ties to the area. I wanted to write up an item in our *Register* about his life and the library memorial, even though he was technically a Bright Bender."

"That's very nice," Ruby praised. "Especially since people in Bright Bend think that you Royal Benders act like you're better than them."

"Oh, we're always going to act that way," Jeff laughed. "We're terribly condescending. We might even put that our welcoming sign: WE REALLY ARE BETTER THAN BRIGHT BEND."

It was a pleasant and chatty ride back to Ruby's, though Jeff dropped her off without much longing or innuendo, only commenting that he'd stop by when he was through visiting with Henry. In truth he was suddenly almost abrupt, evasive, and no longer making steady eye contact, and when the sun set and it became nine and then ten o'clock and he still didn't show up for his promised visit, Ruby began to wonder if she'd misread all his behavior and he wasn't The Man. She lost her relaxed, confident indifference from earlier and grew irritated and confused instead. How dare he skip out when he'd specifically said he would come by, and why couldn't she keep from seeing those calm green eyes and having a strange feeling that she'd be looking into them for many years, over breakfasts and arguments and while lying close together in bed.

It was like a sureness yet completely unsure and it made her want to scream; she snuck out in the dark to spy on Henry Gwynn's place instead and see whether Jeff's car was parked out front. Once she confirmed that Jeff had left, she would let out a nice cleansing shriek into a pillow and begin hating him, but until then she would just be pacing around and waiting pathetically. Right as she reached the dirt road at the end of her driveway, however, Jeff swooped around the corner in his four-door and nearly ran her over. She jumped into a rain ditch to get out of the way while he clambered out from behind the wheel and hauled her back to her feet.

"Good Christ, you scared me!" he yelled. "Are you okay?"

"I'm fine," she said, though her palms had been scraped in the fall and she could see some blood oozing out in the moonlight. Fortunately, he didn't seem to care why she had been outside slinking around and only expressed concern that she wash and bandage the scrapes and that they weren't too deep.

"Sorry to be so late but Henry was talking up a streak and I didn't want to cut him off," Jeff explained. "I don't think I've ever heard him gab so much. So I just waited until he wound down and fell asleep. Only now I'm about ready to nod off myself and I've still got a thirty minute trip back to Royal Bend."

"Would you like some coffee before you go?" Ruby said. She was back to being at ease once more, having looked into his glimmerglass eyes again and felt how he'd pulled her toward him when he'd helped her out of the ditch. It had been a mighty pull followed by an exceptionally close hug.

"I cannot think of anything I'd want more from you than coffee," he smiled back. "Or perhaps I could think of another thing or two, but I know you're a decent young woman."

"Ha," Ruby said, grinding up some coffee beans. "Maybe yes, maybe no."

"And while we're on the subject," he continued, edging up behind her at the sink, which was of course the romantic hotspot of the house. "My Cousin Henry told me that he's seen several gentleman callers stopping by. But he added that you're still a sweet girl and not a hussy."

"Ha," Ruby repeated, now setting the coffee pot on the stovetop. "Maybe yes, maybe no."

He smiled again. "Don't keep saying maybe this or that," he warned. "Unless you're ready to back up your words."

He moved in close so that they were nearly nose to nose and there was a delicious feeling of possibility, but Ruby sensed that it was too possible and sidestepped her way toward the table.

"Maybe I'm not so ready to back those words up after all," she laughed, taking a seat.

Jeff joined her and sat in the opposite chair. "Darn it to all damn," he sighed. "I was hoping to find myself a hussy who can make strong coffee. Though it smells like the coffee won't disappoint me."

"It won't," Ruby said. "I hate weak coffee and weak character."

His eyes widened. "Good one!" he praised. "And I like girls named Ruby with dark hair. What do you think of that?"

"Do you meet many girls named Ruby with dark hair?"

"Not often enough," he said. "I met one back in 1916, one in 1921 and now you. Seems like you're spacing yourself out at intervals. By the way, how old are you? Twenty-three skidoo?"

"Add six to your present total sum," Ruby advised.

"No joke?" he asked. "So heading towards thirty then, but rounding the corner with grace. I just sped by forty myself. In August, which links me with Leo the Lion astrologically." He made clawing gestures at the air and pretended to roar. "I helped out a wacky lady in Boston with some legal matters once and she couldn't afford to pay me, so she read my zodiac chart instead. Told me all about the zodiac too. More than I ever wanted to know. When were you born?"

"June 17th."

He nodded. "You're a Gemini. That seems right too, since you're sort of airy and you like to banter and read and you've had all those gentleman callers. But your birthdate's near the next sign, Cancer the Crab, so you can also be a homebody and caring and offer coffee to weary travelers."

Ruby poured him the coffee in question, which he drank piping hot and black.

"Splendid," he proclaimed. "So what do you think of me," he asked, after a few more long and appreciative sips. "I'm quite the ball of yarn, I'm sure. And I'm in awful shape because I endured a divorce recently, though my wife and I are still chummy and we'd been flailing for years, so it's not like anything was a surprise. But I'll warn you, I don't know whether I'm coming or going sometimes. Well, I do know I'll be going soon from here," he reasoned. "Since I was hoping to get back to Royal Bend and write the weekly issue tonight."

"I thought you only put out the paper if you didn't have anything better to do," Ruby teased, but he tossed that right back at her.

"Then give me something better to do," he prompted. "It's late, we're alone, we have a badminton racket." He leaned over and examined the badminton racket she had taken out of the closet the other day and propped up by the icebox. "Do you use this to strain noodles maybe?"

"I thought there was a mouse in the kitchen so I grabbed that to defend myself," Ruby said. "He turned out to be very cute, though, so I just gave him some cheese and hustled him out into the yard. Or hustled her out. I don't know if it was a female mouse."

"Girl mice wear tiny pink bows in their fur, I believe," Jeff said. "And hoop skirts. So how are you at this badminton game?"

"I'd probably beat you," Ruby assessed. "I beat most people. Alma and Jasper won't even play with me anymore because I'm too vicious. They want badminton to be fun and leisurely and I keep slamming the shuttlecock into their faces."

Jeff poured another cup of coffee, drank it down, then set the cup and saucer in the sink. He extended his hand to Ruby and told her to walk him to the car.

"How about a picnic tomorrow?" he asked. "Take the train up to meet me and I'll introduce you to some folks, then you and I can bring a basket of food and some badminton rackets into the woods and see what transpires. I'll pay your fare. I'd drive back here to get you but if you make the trip there I can sneak in a few hours' work. I work a lot," he warned. "I practice law in Binghamton and Royal Bend, then I write the *Register* and go to civic meetings and lodge meetings and meetings about meetings and family things."

"Yet you want to spend your Sunday with me," Ruby said. "I feel so honored and special."

"And you should!" he joked, yet then he continued more anxiously. "So is it possible? Or if not this Sunday then next Sunday—or some other Sunday." He held her by the arms with mock melodrama. "Just give me one Sunday with a dark-haired Ruby before I meet the next one in 1936."

"But the world's going to end on March 3, 1933," Ruby said. "You know, 3-3-33. A man dressed in black like an undertaker stopped me on Market Street and gave me the news last summer. He was like the Angel of Death, eating a dill pickle."

Jeff laughed. "Why shouldn't the Angel of Death enjoy a pickle every now and then? By the way, I like your sense of humor—meaning that you have one. And this cottage of yours looks much nicer since you took it over. I always meant to stop by and say hello, but Cousin Henry's only been back in the family circle for a couple of months and it's been a busy summer. I also wouldn't want to compete with your other suitors. Any of them lurking around right now?"

"Sure, they're lurking all over—smoking, playing cards, polishing their ducling pistols. Or just taking naps," Ruby said

"Don't say the words nap or sleep or fatigue or slumber or snoring," Jeff complained. "Not unless you want me to nod off and drive into a tree. Although at least there won't be much traffic at this hour," he considered, brightening somewhat. He contemplated Ruby further, then moved close toward her like he had before, but again there was no kiss or significant contact. He seemed to be sniffing at her hair instead.

"Rosewater?" he guessed, smelling all those crushed petals from her steamy rose bath.

"Roses and water, yes," she said.

"Do you always smell like roses?" he asked. "Should I start calling you Rose instead? No, a Ruby is not a Rose by any other name," he resolved. "So I'll meet you at the station tomorrow around noon-ish? If I'm not there it's because I fell asleep at my desk in my office, which is next to the barbershop. So walk on over and come poke me with a stick."

Ruby picked up a branch off the ground. "I've got the stick."

After another minute of tense stalling and indecision, Jeff turned quickly, revved up his car and hurried off. Without so much as a final word or a handshake, or even a toot of the horn. Ruby went back into the house and locked the door, then sat on the couch in the dark thinking about how even though this spell was officially finished, she still seemed to be in for more twists in the road. More twists, more uncertainty, more unsettling men. She had half a mind not to meet him tomorrow and just head back to Philadelphia. She'd given it the summer and that was enough—and she was also sick of the smell of roses hanging around her person and got up to take a bath and use plain old sensible Ivory soap instead.

In the morning when her wind-up alarm clock trilled, Ruby turned it off, stared at the botanical print of violets on the wall and decided to go back to sleep. The summer had begun with the pressed violets in Aunt May's letter urging her to try the spell, and three months later she was still looking at violets with a muddled head. Like she had been thinking last night, enough was enough—no more violets, pinecones, honey, pies, hyssop, locks of hair, nettles or soggy roses. Just delectably meaningless sleep.

She was falling back into drowsy peace again, however, when she heard Sweetie clucking and Aunt May calling from the kitchen. Aunt May had a spare key and if she stopped by for an extra egg or two from Sweetie, she sometimes would let herself in and start making breakfast. It smelled like she was flipping pancakes down there and Ruby hadn't eaten since the Reading Room party, so hunger won out over sleep and she slipped on her robe and went to join her. Aunt May was all fresh and spry in a leaf-green dress and lilac apron and Ruby smiled at the sight.

"Aren't you adorable," she said.

"Why, thank you. And aren't you supposed to be to meeting Jeff Bryce soon?" Aunt May asked. "Here's your coffee and flapjacks and maple or huckleberry syrup—take your pick. Then after you've eaten you'd better shake a leg."

"No leg shaking today," Ruby yawned, opting for huckleberry syrup for one half of her pancake stack and maple for the other. The maple syrup was tapped locally and was so thick and pure and delicious that Ruby had to take a plain bite of pancake to neutralize the taste so that she could fully savor the tartly sweet huckleberry version. "I'm not going. It's September 22nd. There's a chill in the air, nights are longer, and I've lost the summer love fever. And how did you even know I was supposed to meet Jeff Bryce?"

"Your chicken told me. And don't be silly about not going. The spell worked and now you just have to gather the harvest," Aunt May said, and what was funniest was that she was utterly serious.

"Sorry, I thought it worked too but this crop's not ready to be harvested. Or it has weevils," Ruby said. "Jeff even admitted himself that he doesn't know if he's coming or going, so let's let him sort that all out on his own. Will you watch Sweetie if I head back to Philadelphia? I'll visit once a month, but I need to find a new job and check on my apartment and get into the swing of things there again. And when I say watch Sweetie I mean *don't eat her*. If you put her in a stewpot I'll never come up here anymore."

"I won't eat your silly hen," Aunt May promised. "She lays twice as many eggs as my own birds and I've got a rooster I was hoping to mate her with. That'll probably happen easier than finding a mate for you."

"I don't doubt that," Ruby concurred. Aunt May dropped a square of lard into the skillet to make another batch of pancakes and it sizzled crisply. "Aunt May, I've got plenty here. No more for me, or are you fixing those for yourself?"

"They're for Jeff Bryce," Aunt May replied matter of factly. "He didn't drive back to Royal Bend last night, he knew he was too tired and turned the car around and stayed with his Cousin Henry. I happen to know this because I've been taking care of Henry myself for about two months, ever since you told me he stole your strawberry pie. It seemed like he'd gotten himself into a pitiful state over there so I let bygones be bygones and started to help him clean up and eat better. Henry and I were friends once so many years ago and we let pride get in the way, but we're older and maybe wiser now and we have shared memories of a time that not many others remember. And Jeff Bryce knows I've been visiting Henry, but I didn't want anyone else to know just yet and Jeff's respected my wishes. He's a whip-smart, nice-looking young man with prospects and he's also clever enough to keep you happy. I told him about the Reading Room party because I knew he was the best match for you."

"I thought Ben was your favorite," Ruby teased.

Aunt May smiled guiltily. "Ben is my favorite, I can't lie. But I put my own hopes before yours and I wasn't thinking of who you are and what you need in a husband, and that's why you and Ben were like a batch of jelly that never set firm. Now let me ask you another thing—were you aware that Henry Gwynn's asked me to marry him?

"Not at all!" Ruby replied, both shocked and even somewhat unnerved by the notion. Because you had wonderful clean and lovely Aunt May, and then you had dingy sooty hunched-over Henry Gwynn. "Are you going to accept?"

"I don't believe so," Aunt May said quietly. "Only because when and if I make my way up to Heaven and our Lord, I want to be there only as Zerah Campbell's wife. He was my true love and I should respect his memory. But it's my Christian duty and even my pleasure to help my friend Henry along."

"Aunt May," Ruby noted. "You shouldn't say *if* I make my way to Heaven and our Lord, because if you're not headed up there then no one else is."

"That's not our decision, dear," Aunt May demurred. "Now what I meant to mention is that Jeff Bryce has respected my wishes in not telling you about the marriage proposal either. He could have been gossipy or joked about how now there'll be two sets of dentures in one glass every night, but he kept quiet and that adds to his integrity."

"Don't you still have nearly all your own teeth?" Ruby wondered, but Aunt May argued that Jeff Bryce *could* have made that sort of joke and he hadn't.

"You ought to give it one more day," Aunt May urged. "He's right here ready to take you for a drive to anywhere you'd like—he said that himself when I stopped by an hour ago. I'll bet he'd even drive you back to Philadelphia if you insist on going there. He just wanted to shave and wash up, and since he's at Henry's that might take awhile. I've cleaned that pig sty somewhat, but I've got a ways to go."

"I ought to make him drive me back to Philadelphia," Ruby muttered.

"Give Jeff one more day," Aunt May persisted. "Unless you really don't care for him," she said. "It wouldn't be fair to string him along if you have no interest at all. But I think you like him, Ruby. And he's part-Greek, for goodness sakes! Here you are with your spice jars and foreign recipes and here's a nearly foreign fellow himself."

He's also nearly a man from a faraway land, Ruby thought, remembering the fortuneteller at the Fair. Even though the same man had been at the same Fair judging a pie contest in seersucker, which wasn't exactly exotic— but he did have a shadow of dashing Greek darkness to him, Ruby had to admit. And now he was at the back door, wearing yesterday's suit and shirt yet otherwise appearing freshly-washed and terribly shaved.

"Sorry to look like this," he said, gingerly touching the various cuts and scrapes on his cheeks and chin. "But Cousin Henry's only got a straight razor and I'm out of practice with them. I think he also uses his to saw wood. Worst blade on earth."

"We ought to get him a new razor then," Aunt May suggested. "And a new comb and brush. I'll have Alma pick some things out."

"Be sure to send the bill to me," Jeff insisted. "You shouldn't have to pay for all that, May."

Aunt May beamed over such generosity and gave Ruby a significant glance. She then ordered Ruby to get dressed and not be lolling around in her robe while company was over.

Jeff sat before his own plate of pancakes and gave Ruby another significant glance. "I have no issue with you being in your robe and if you'd like to loll, please do."

"No, she should not," Aunt May bristled. "It isn't proper—scoot and get changed, Ruby."

Ruby sighed, then took her coffee cup into her room and went through her morning routine while Aunt May fussed over Jeff Bryce. Now Aunt May was going to be all stuck on Jeff; she'd switched one big bumblebee in her bonnet for another. While Ruby was stepping into her slip, however, she saw the single red rose in the east window from the night before last and how it still looked fresh and hadn't dropped any petals yet. She heard Jeff laughing about something with Aunt May and she smiled along with them herself, because he had an infectious laugh, and it occurred to her suddenly yet thoughtfully that if he kept taking three strides forward then two back, she ought to not be doing the same. She was on her guard as much as he was, but even with all the summer's revolving door of suitors, she hadn't gone through as much as he had. She hadn't suffered through a divorce or had her heart wrung out or even particularly bruised.

Ruby stared at the rose, and then the print of violets, and then the rose again. The right thing to do would be to give Jeff Bryce another chance as Aunt May had proposed, but damn it, she was just fractious now and in need of a break from Bright Bend and Royal Bend and all the bends around. She really wanted a few days in Philadelphia on her own and if this pairing was so celestial and meant to be, it surely could continue once she came back.

She packed a few essentials, then put on the dress that she'd been taking all summer to finish sewing— the one that Ben Greenlee had thought was too racy and low-cut. She had come up with her own design, piecing together a brown silk skirt, pink silk paisley top and black velvet edging at the neck. Jeff didn't appear to have the same decency issues as Aunt May's other ideal.

"No wonder you want to hurry back to Philadelphia," he whistled. "You're hoping to show off that outfit."

"I made it," Ruby said.

"Then you should open a shop."

"Hardly," she laughed. "It took me months to sew one dress and I still haven't bound the seams. Not that you can tell, but Aunt May would be disgusted. Where is she anyhow?"

"At church, then she'll be back over to Henry's to fix Sunday dinner," Jeff said. "Boy, he's lucky that for some miraculous reason she decided to take care of him. Incredibly lucky."

"Aunt May honestly loves caring for people," Ruby speculated. "That makes her feel lucky and fulfilled too. Her husband's passed away, her son and grandchildren live in St. Louis, her daughter's extremely capable and even I'm independent enough. But Henry needs her, and like she told me before, they're the same age and they've been through things together even though they've led separate lives."

Jeff appeared to be having one of his turtle into the shell moments and kept quiet, staring down at the tablecloth with his lips pursed. Rather than being annoyed, Ruby waited it out instead this time and he indeed did move past the moody silence. He looked up and gazed at her steadily.

"What would you like to do today?" he asked. "Assuming that a sharp number like yourself wants to be seen with a man in a wrinkled suit who looks like he shaved with the lid of a tin can."

"You just look intriguingly rumpled," Ruby said. "Like you've been at one of Gatsby's all-night parties. And I'm afraid that I am going to have to take this dress and myself to Philadelphia for a short while. It's time for a change of scenery. I'll be back soon, though. Would you mind driving me to the station?"

He agreed immediately, without any protest, and didn't seem troubled in the least that she was leaving town. She phoned Alma and asked her or Aunt May to take care of the chicken, and then she said goodbye to Sweetie and gave her a kiss on the head before putting her in her coop with an ear of corn. Sweetie didn't like being in the coop in general, but she would tolerate it if she had something to snack on.

"Have you always been fond of chickens?" Jeff inquired, still not at ease around Sweetie—and that situation was mutual. Ruby explained that the chicken had been a gift from Ned Whist and that Sweetie was not for consumption.

"Giving a girl a chicken instead of a box of chocolates—how original. And practical," he noted. "But then not every woman wants a chicken. Most prefer the box of candy, or a bunch of flowers, or just a goldfish. What do you think about a live turkey? Should I bring you one of those next time I come calling?"

"Only if you sing *Turkey in the Straw* too," Ruby said.

She waited in the passenger seat of his car while he checked his tires and wiped dust from the dirt roads off the windshield with a rag. It was turning into a golden, mellow day with a light wind and random milkweed puffs floating by. Jeff finally got behind the wheel and smiled vaguely. She smiled vaguely back.

"That's not a bad look for you," she said. "A little worse for the wear. Makes you seem kind of—what's the word?"

"Seedy?"

"No."

"Hideous?"

"Try raffish instead."

His green eyes lit up at the idea of raffishness and he touched her hand. His touch was hesitant at first, but he moved on to holding her hand until he was ready to crank-start the engine. He then drove steadily toward the train station; he slowed the car as they approached the railroad crossing yet sped up as it disappeared behind them.

"Why aren't you stopping?" Ruby asked. "My train's due in twelve minutes."

"True, but you won't be on it," he said. "I'm kidnapping you and taking you on a picnic. Your Aunt May told me to do it, so she's my accomplice."

"Oh, the hell with you both," Ruby sighed, starting to feel more trapped than she cared for.

"Such language!" Jeff objected. "I have no problem with you cussing at me but spare that darling little lady."

"Darling sneaky little lady," Ruby said, considering a surprise takeover of the car but she hadn't driven in so long that she'd most likely end up locking all the gears.

"You don't want to hop that train anyhow, because it'll be crowded and noisy and full of Sunday yahoos. Besides, Philadelphia's been around for a while and I suspect it may still be there tomorrow. But today we'll stop for sandwiches and find some idyllic picnic spot," Jeff promised. "Aunt May fetched your other badminton racket so we've got both of those in the trunk. Just like our original plan."

"Whoopee," Ruby answered flatly, though she did have to admit it was especially fine picnicking weather.

"Now don't be sullen," he admonished. "I know this is one of the oldest tricks in the book but you stepped into my vehicle and that made you fair game. And that's why it's in the book, because it's a time-tested trick that works. And in case you weren't aware, it's my birthday and I'd rather not spend it alone."

"Liar," she scoffed. "You already told me you'd had your birthday in August, Leo the Lion."

He winced. "Why did I mention that and why were you even listening? I'm going to have to be careful around you," he observed. "Unlike most Geminis, you pay attention."

They were on the side roads because the highway tended to be mobbed on Sundays, and after about ten rattling miles north, Jeff stopped the car and wiped the windshield again.

"I must seem somewhat distant," he said suddenly, like they had been having a conversation all along. "And raffish," he laughed. "But I've spent a couple of years meeting the wrong kind of women and holding up my defenses since my wife and I ended things. I mean the wrong kind of women being sent my way through my family and friends, not the *wrong kind* of women like vamps and floozies and other men's wives. These were all stellar individuals, but they weren't right for me. Though my wife wasn't right for me either," he reflected. "But that's because she was too much—too vivacious, too energetic, and too tall really. She's stunning and talented and when she left me for a journalist who wanted to travel all over the planet, I came to realize how it was all for the best. I was barely able to handle living and lawyering in Boston—that's where she's originally from. I'd kept up with her when we were younger and both had big plans, but my big plans became too small and hers never changed." He sighed. "We're great friends still. She just sent me a paperweight from Italy."

Ruby reached over and touched his hand this time, moving her fingers over the tips of his squarely narrow nails.

"I didn't mean to say that you were anything less than she was," he added hastily. "You're not anything less—you're even more, in your own way. It's so difficult having to pick and choose words. I never had problems like this before and I only have them now when I'm talking to women."

"I'm sure it'll get easier," Ruby said, letting down her own defenses again. "Right now you have to tell me lots of things and then I'll have to tell you about my life, and then we'll have to kiss or not kiss or see each other again or not see each other."

He nodded. "You'll have to come to Royal Bend and meet my mother and aunt and uncle, and they'll check your hair and teeth and the size of your hips to see if you're good breeding stock. But if you like food from other countries you'll enjoy the Sunday dinner at least. Stuffed grape leaves, spinach pie, egg and lemon soup, pastries with nuts and fig cookies."

"Yes to all that," Ruby agreed. "That'll make the breeding stock part worthwhile."

"Then there's the other side," he said. "Don't forget that my dear departed father was a Susquehanna County man. Who happened to look a lot like Buffalo Bill."

Ruby shrugged her shoulders. "I'm used to Susquehannans. And hopefully somebody on that end will have a good gingerbread recipe because Aunt May's has too much molasses for my taste."

A few other cars passed them on the road, whipping up a wind that sent a few extra copies of the *Royal Bend Register* flapping around the backseat.

"What does your middle initial stand for?" Ruby asked, helping to gather up the loose issues and noting his name on the front page. "The M of Jefferson M. Bryce."

"Molasses," Jeff said. "No, it's Makarios. That means fortunate or blessed in Greek. So much for names!"

"I can truly say I would have never guessed that," Ruby replied. "And you haven't written this week's paper yet—you never got back to your office yesterday."

"You gave me something better to do," Jeff said. "Though I did think up one of the quips you like so much, after I almost hit you with the car when I was coming over from Cousin Henry's: *As the poet Byron wrote, she walks in beauty, like the night...so be careful or you might run her over on a dark road.*"

"Love it," Ruby declared. "It's a dream come true, being part of the *Royal Bend Register*'s weekly quips."

"Is that sarcasm?"

"Not totally."

"How about sandwiches?"

"Are they sarcastic?"

"No, but as I mentioned before, they're needed for a picnic," Jeff continued, restarting the engine. "Followed by badminton and assorted licentious activities."

"I know what licentious means and just because you put me in your newspaper doesn't mean you can get fresh, Mister," Ruby teased, and he laughed and they resumed their dusty course.

They bought sandwiches at a roadhouse-type restaurant near Tulip Tree Lake, called not surprisingly the Tulip Tree Inn, with a friendly cook who knew Jeff from Binghamton and who put together their picnic lunch right away. The cook was a broad, towering man with a face like a hatchet and an unusually gentle voice. He gave them roast beef sandwiches with horseradish and mayonnaise, devilled eggs, coleslaw, potato salad, oatmeal cookies and an apple. Jeff had requested the apple.

"Nature's toothbrush," he explained.

Evidently within an hour the place would be packed and it would stay packed like it was every Sunday from spring until autumn. They had just beat the crowds but the cook and his hostess sister and a waitress were running around making last-minute preparations. Ruby asked to use the restaurant restroom to freshen up and get some of the road dirt off her face, and she was glad to see that a new bar of soap was in the dish and the towels were dry and clean. She was finishing her toilette and washing her hands when she noticed that the china soap dish had a painted figure in its center, and that that figure was a dragonfly.

"There it is," she marveled, peering at herself in the mirror and wondering whether it was just the dim light or did she really look so warmly happy and dewy-eyed.

Jeff of course had no idea about the dragonfly dream and instead filled her in on how Archibald the cook had once been in trouble for throwing a cinderblock through a department store window in Binghamton while drunk, but Jeff had managed to get the charges reduced from theft to disorderly conduct. Archie had cooled his heels in jail for a mere week, then been released and had since stayed away from liquor and cinderblocks.

"I always try to pay him for sandwiches and meals but he won't take a dime," Jeff said. "His sister's the brains and hustle behind this place and she'll take money from me, but Archie gives her hell afterward. She's entitled to it by now, though. I've had two years of free meals there."

"My father used to do things like that," Ruby smiled.

"Well, there are times to be heartless if you're a lawyer and then there are times to be charitable," Jeff said. "Archie's mother cleans my office in Binghamton and she gave me the sob story of what had happened, and it took me less than an hour to work out a defense and make one court appearance. Seemed worth it to give a big lummox a second chance."

They kept on toward Tulip Tree Lake—which technically had more pines than tulip trees, or even tulips—on a rocky path suited better for a mule than a car, but somehow they were able to park by a pine glade and meander toward the water. Ruby remembered this lake from years back, having come here with Andrew J. to go fishing. She had only been about nine and it was one of her rare visits to her father's old haunts; he had taken her out on a rowboat and seemed oddly at peace simply catching pike, then throwing them back. Ruby had been thrilled to spend so much time with him and watch the usual grayness seep from his face, but unfortunately he had insisted that she keep quiet most of the day so as not to disturb the fish or him, and that had not been easy for her at that age. The lake had had only wobbly cabins then but now it was flanked with spacious summer homes and gleaming freshly-painted docks. She and Jeff did not go near the homes, since they were private property and marked against trespassing, but they did find a high ground that was flat and meadowy.

"Do you like living here?" Jeff asked after they had finished almost everything that Archibald had given them, except for the apple. "Or do you miss the city?"

"I miss certain things about city life," she admitted. "But I'm not unhappy now. If I stayed in Bright Bend I'd like to visit the city twice a month or so. Or vice versa. Why did you move back? Didn't you like Boston?"

"I liked it until my wife left," he said. "I was only there because of her, but I did find my own friends and interesting colleagues. I was thinking of moving to Philadelphia for a change of scene after she, uh, decamped—but I had my tenth law school reunion at Cornell and took a long vacation visiting my family afterward, since I had to pass through Royal Bend anyway. I'd always wanted to get out of town when I was younger and set some corner of the world on fire, but at that point it seemed like there were opportunities back home that I ought to consider. Royal Bend's lawyer had retired and I became reacquainted with an old law school buddy who needed a partner in Binghamton—and it was all just like fruit dropping into my lap. I'd been out on a lot of limbs scrambling for fruit beforehand, so I was happy to take it."

"We might have met in Philadelphia if you'd gone there instead," she noted.

"We might, but more likely on a streetcar or over spiked punch and shrimp puffs at someone's apartment. It would have been all citified and proper and we wouldn't be in such a lovely place like we are now," he said. "This is a slice. On ground that's damp and chilly, but still a slice."

He was lying on the blanket they had unfolded with his suit jacket off, his shirtsleeves rolled up and shirttail untucked. He appeared on the verge of falling asleep, which was why she was surprised to see him bound up and insist on playing badminton instead. After she shook off her own afternoon grog, they went at it.

They flipped a coin for the serve and Ruby won. He shrugged indifferently and paced back to his part of the meadowy playing field, and so the game began. About an hour later, they called it a draw out of sheer exhaustion and admiration for each other. Ruby had learned that he was as crazed as she was when holding a badminton racket, and just as prone to slam a shuttlecock into the other player's collarbone or face, or to keep said other player running from side to side then racing backwards or diving forward to reach the lightest tap of a shot. Jeff then reached out as if to shake her hand, but he laughed and dragged her down onto the blanket again instead.

She laughed too until he gave her a careful but exploratory kiss, while his right hand ventured along her bare left leg. They proceeded slowly but intensely for about as long as they had played badminton, but with more unified and cooperative motion. Then Ruby felt blissfully tired and just couldn't kiss or touch anymore, and she lay back listening to some late season cicadas whirring in the distance while Jeff put himself to rights and tucked his shirt back in.

"So where's this headed?" he prompted.

Ruby opened and closed her eyes so that her lashes made a dark screen against the bright sky and sun.

"I think it's going someplace," she offered. "At least until I get that Greek dinner you promised."

"Then the diabolical kidnapping plan has succeeded," he said. "Along with the promise of moussaka and spanokopita. And speaking of bewaring almost-Greeks bearing gifts—" He took the apple out of the grocery box they had used to hold their picnic lunch, slicing it with a pocket knife and offering her half. She accepted and chewed thoughtfully; it was a crisp, juicy yellow-skinned variety, with something like both an apple and pear taste. Jeff ate his half as well, and when she had finished he kissed the remaining juice from her fingertips.

"Now you're really done for," he announced.

She yawned and admired the touches of red and orange just starting to color the mountain trees surrounding the lake. "Why, was it a poisoned apple?" she asked.

"No, but it had a spell on it," he said. "One of the oldest love spells there is, going back to Aphrodite. You might call the goddess of love Venus, but we Greeks call her Aphrodite and Aphrodite creates aphrodisiacs. All you have to do is get an apple, cut it in half, and offer it to the person of interest. If that person takes the apple and eats it and you eat your half, it's a closed deal."

"Is it that easy?" Ruby said, trying not to roll around the ground in hysterical convulsions. "I thought that love spells were complicated. Like you have to keep track of waxing and waning moons and bathe in the morning dew and follow precise steps," she added, of course not wanting to disclose any of the secret rituals that seemingly could have been replaced by one single apple. But then again, Ruby sensed that their magic apple had taken all summer to grow and ripen and make its way to this very spot, and probably through her own personal spell malarkey, so had she.

He was frowning and mulling over her last remark. "I'm not sure how complicated love spells are," he said. "There are different kinds from different cultures, though, and I've heard of some even being conjured up around here."

"Love spells being conjured around here? No! You're kidding?" Ruby gasped.

He nodded sagely. "So goes the rumor. My mother used the apple trick on my father and here I am along with my two sisters. Of course, he was so gaga he would have married her if she'd given him a wormy potato. And you're not really bound to this—I'm sure I could write you up a document to void the contract, then we'd just have to send it to Mount Olympus or at least Washington, D.C. Let me know if you want to escape."

"I will," she said, smiling at his green eyes searching hers and his long straight nose and appealingly scratched-up face. She then lay her head on his shoulder and watched huge cottonball clouds move across the sky while the lake water lapped and sighed below, and the pines filled the air with sharp scent and the sun filled the air with hazy light—and two apple core husks lay on the ground, all making it truly a perfect first day of fall.

From the *Twin Bend Chronicle* — July 17, 1988

❁

We would like to note the passing of Ruby Pritchard Bryce last month, a few days after her 88th birthday. Ruby was my second cousin and I always enjoyed looking into her lively brown eyes, hearing her happy laugh, or tasting some peppery Moroccan stew she'd just cooked up. Ruby loved the spice of life and even wrote a book about the history of spices featuring her favorite recipes, and that same book's been in print for over twenty years. Her daughter Lila is as pretty as she was and—until my wife distracted me with her own beauteous presence—I must say I was one of the boys hanging around the station waiting for Lila's train whenever she made visits home from college. And my twin grand-girls can't seem to live without Ruby's granddaughter Fleur's appropriately flowery fashion design creations.

Ruby was contentedly married to Jeff Bryce until his death in 1982, and we all know Jeff as the smart man who headed the *Royal Bend Register*, untangled our legal snarls, and rallied with success to keep both Bright Bend and Royal Bend from losing their historic charm. Jeff was a pal of my father's and about as quick-witted and charming, but as the story goes it was Ruby's earlier sweetheart Pete Nickels who came up this way for a visit in the summer of 1929 and had my parents cavorting so much with his piano playing and accompanying cocktails that some nine months later, I was born. (You could never tell that slightly risqué tale with my mother in the room, but my father Jasper would recount it proudly to whoever cared to listen.) And that's why my name is Pete.

On one other occasion, I made a trip to Philadelphia with Cousin Ruby and we bought her spices and fabric and me my first portable typewriter. Then we met a skinny fellow with a goatee at the art museum and he and Ruby chuckled over old times. He showed her a painting of a wispy girl on one of the museum walls and she gave him a sack of coins. That man was the artist Eli Baird Turnby, and the girl in the painting was Cousin Ruby standing by Tyler's Creek. She insisted that she'd had more clothing on then than she did in the painting, though when Mr. Turnby asked if Ruby resented being transformed into a near-naked nymph, Cousin Ruby said she didn't mind as much as she once might have because it was nice to see how "well put together" she used to be.

We have an Eli Turnby watercolor in the Bright Bend Library now, and while he reportedly painted that scene for a couple of shaving items and ten bucks, I understand his stuff fetches far more at auction nowadays.

It's a shame that Ruby missed the arrival of summer, which was always her favorite season. And it seems like we'll have a pleasant one this year, if the recent temperatures and sunny skies are any prediction. Just curiously, it's always interesting to note how one can spot locks of hair hanging from ribbons on trees around this area in July, here and there, and only for a short time. Might be some sorority ritual but I've never gotten any real answers as to what that business is all about, and, like much in the world, it makes me wonder.

Pete Darby, Editor